Sadie Rose

AND THE OUTLAW RUSTLERS

A PRAIRIE FAMILY ADVENTURE

Sadie Rose
AND THE
OUTLAW RUSTLERS

Hilda Stahl

CROSSWAY BOOKS • WHEATON, ILLINOIS
A DIVISION OF GOOD NEWS PUBLISHERS

*Dedicated with love and
special thanks
to
Norman Stahl*

Sadie Rose and the Outlaw Rustlers. Copyright © 1989 by Hilda Stahl. Published by Crossway Books, a division of Good News Publishers, Wheaton, Illinois 60187.

Cover illustration: Kathy Kulin

Fourth printing, 1991

Printed in the United States of America

Library of Congress Catalog Card Number 89-50331

ISBN 0-89107-528-3

Contents

1

Sadie's New Room

Careful not to wake Helen or Opal, Sadie eased off the bed. Her heart leaped, and she wanted to dance across the cool, damp, hard-packed dirt floor. She stepped to the window and touched the glass. It was real glass. "Our very own bedroom window," she said under her breath. For over two months they'd slept in the covered wagon, but yesterday and the day before the neighbors had come over to help build a sod house big enough for all seven of them.

She touched the still-damp sod that Riley had cut with a plow from the vast Nebraska prairie. It smelled like a freshly plowed garden. She felt a root, but she didn't pull it out because a chunk of sod would come with it, leaving a hole in the wall.

A shadow moved under Momma's tree, and Sadie knew it was Tanner keeping watch over the homestead. Maybe he'd heard a coyote yip, but he wouldn't bark at coyotes unless they got too close to Bossie and her calf or the horses. He stepped out in the moonlight and faced the north, his flag of a tail still for once.

How could anyone sleep on such a wonderful night? The moon shone almost bright as day. The warm May wind blew, but couldn't blow into the tight sod house.

Sadie rubbed her hand gently down the sheeting that she'd helped Momma and Opal hang in the bedroom to turn it into three bedrooms—one for sixteen-year-old Riley and eight-year-old Webster, one for her, Opal, and Helen, and one for Momma and Caleb York, their new father.

Sadie touched a peg stuck in the thick sod—a peg that was hers alone. Opal and Helen had pegs of their own, and she didn't have to share hers with anyone. Both her dresses hung on it. In the moonlight it was impossible to tell that her everyday dress was old and patched or that her blue gingham good dress had tiny stitches down the front where Opal had carefully sewn up the terrible tear caused by Tanner's toenail.

With her bare toe she touched her crate that held her own personal things. Would she ever own a chest of drawers like Mable Proctor had back in Douglas County? Sadie frowned. She should be thankful for her very own wonderful crate and not wish for something she didn't need.

She bent down to the crate, then listened to make sure Helen and Opal were still asleep. She heard low snores from Riley and louder snores from Caleb. He said he didn't snore, but Momma had laughed and told him he did.

Sadie frowned as she remembered how Caleb had grabbed Momma tight in his arms and kissed her right in front of all of them, even eight-year-old Helen. Helen hadn't even turned red, but Sadie knew *she* had. She'd looked away, but not before she'd seen the happy glow on Momma's face. In all the years Momma had been married to Pa before he'd died in the blizzard, not once had Pa kissed her in front of others. Once in a while he'd touch her soft brown hair or run a finger down her cheek, but that was it.

But now Pa was in Heaven, his body was buried back in Douglas County, and they were here at the edge of the sandhills with Caleb York as their daddy.

Sadie flicked away a tear and slowly reached into her crate and under her underwear for Holly, her rag doll that she'd made from scraps and stuffed with pieces of rags that Momma couldn't use for anything else. Being a big girl of twelve, she knew she was too old to play with dolls. But Holly was more than a doll—Holly was her friend.

She touched the embroidered eyes, then hugged her close against her soft nightgown that was almost too small for her. The day before yesterday, for the first time ever, she'd showed Holly to someone.

Sadie leaned against the wide windowsill and looked off across the prairie where she knew Mary Ferguson lay sleeping. Jewel Comstock, their closest neighbor, had taken Mary in so they'd both have someone. Jewel's husband had died years ago, and Mary was an orphan. Together they were a family.

Day before yesterday Mary had said, "We'll be best friends, Sadie."

"Best friends," said Sadie. She'd never expected

to have a best friend when they'd moved across Nebraska to the edge of the sandhills. "Want to see my doll?" She'd taken Mary to the pile of stuff under the heavy canvas from the covered wagon, and when she'd made sure no one was looking she'd introduced Mary to Holly. "But don't tell anyone about her," she'd whispered. "I don't want anybody to tease me."

Mary hugged Holly close. "She's beautiful. She will be friends with Amanda." Amanda was Mary's corncob doll that her ma had made for her before she and the rest of Mary's family had died of a terrible sickness. "I promise not to tell anyone." She had leaned close to Sadie. "Especially not Levi Cass."

Sadie flushed just thinking about it. Levi was sixteen, and he'd think she was indeed a baby if he found out that she had a rag doll. Sadie kissed Holly on the tiny bonnet that she'd stitched herself from a piece of brown gingham.

Helen moved in her sleep and muttered something Sadie couldn't understand. Moonlight made Helen's baby-fine hair look whiter than usual.

Opal flipped onto her side, pulling the light blanket with her. She was fourteen, waiting to be sixteen so she could marry a fine young man and have a home and babies of her own. She had her eye on Levi Cass, but after yesterday she couldn't decide if she wanted to marry him or one of the two bachelors that lived in a dugout on Cottonwood Creek down from Jewel Comstock.

Trembling, Sadie pushed Holly back out of sight in the crate. Opal would tease her and tell everyone if she knew about Holly.

Sadie swallowed, and her mouth felt bone-dry. She crept to the sheeting, eased it aside, and stepped around it and into the kitchen. The smell of fried venison from supper hung in the air. She walked to the washstand that held a bucket of water and the washbasin. She filled the dipper and drank. The cool water felt good against her dry throat. She hung the dipper in place and looked around, the glow of the moonlight making it easy to see. It was hard to get used to the big room. Caleb was building a big table with benches, so they'd all be able to sit down to eat together. Not even in Douglas County had they had a table big enough for all of them. Momma had set plates on a bench and let Helen and Web kneel at it to eat. Sadie had shared a chair with Opal, and they sat at a corner of the table, with Riley, Momma, and Pa squeezed together around the rest of the table. No one spoke while they ate, except Pa if he felt like talking. Usually he didn't.

Sadie turned toward the bedroom, then stopped. A strange feeling rippled over her. She fingered one of her dark braids that hung to her slender shoulders. Maybe she should check on Tanner.

Carefully she lifted the latch and pulled open the heavy door. She left it ajar as she stepped out to the packed ground just outside the door. Stars lit the huge sky, and the wind pressed her nightgown against her thin legs. The leaves on Momma's tree rustled. It was the only tree on Caleb's place. He'd planted it special for Momma as a wedding gift.

Tanner whined as if something were wrong and ran to her side.

"What is it, boy?" she asked softly. Even her whisper sounded loud in the great silence of the prairie.

He rubbed her bare foot with his paw and whined louder.

When a whiff of smoke drifted to her on the wind, Sadie stiffened. Her heart leaped to her mouth, and fear pricked her skin. When she was Helen's age, she'd watched Pa and the neighbors fight a blazing prairie fire that had burned Pa's friend Joel Badger to ashes. The fire had leaped high and then settled down, only to leap high again when the wind gusted. Smoke billowed out from it, and when the fire was finally out Pa had been as black as coal and coughed all night long.

Tanner pawed Sadie's foot again, and she wrapped her arms around his neck and held him tight.

"It can't be a prairie fire, Tanner," she whispered into his neck. She smelled his dusty hair and turned her face away. "It is only my imagination." After the last prairie fire, she'd smelled smoke on the wind and had seen flames leaping on the horizon when neither was really there.

Tanner pulled away from her and stood rigid, looking toward the north.

Her stomach tightened, and she stood beside him and looked again. Was there a red glow or was it her imagination? She groaned. Dare she wake Momma and tell her?

Finally she turned and ran into the house. She stopped just outside the sheet that blocked Momma's bed from view. "Momma," she whispered.

"What's wrong, Sadie Rose?" asked Caleb York instead of Momma.

Sadie bit her bottom lip. "Maybe nothin'." She stood quietly, her heart thudding. "Probably nothin'." She heard a rustling behind the sheeting and Caleb stepped out, wearing only his pants. He clamped a large hand on her shoulder, and she trembled. He was tall and lean, with muscles that rippled under his sun-darkened skin.

"What is it, Sadie Rose?" he asked in a low, gentle Texas drawl.

"I thought I smelled smoke."

He motioned toward the big black stove across the room. "The stove?"

She shook her head. "Outside."

He strode out the door in his bare feet and stood beside Tanner.

Sadie followed him and felt his tension. Would he smell smoke and see the red glow? Or would he laugh at her and tell her to go back to bed where she belonged?

"Get Riley." Caleb's voice snapped as loud as the bullwhip he often used. "It's a fire all right. North of here." He ran back into the house with Sadie on his heels. "It's near that new homestead the bachelors told me about. Tell Riley to get a move on."

Sadie ran to Riley's bed and shook him. Her hand couldn't reach all the way around the muscles in his arm. "Riley, hurry! Prairie fire! Daddy needs you now!"

Riley shot up, immediately awake. "Be right there, Daddy," he called.

Web jumped up. "Me too, Daddy!"

"Not you, Web," said Caleb.

"Me, Daddy?" asked Sadie, her icy hands locked together.

Caleb didn't answer for a while, then finally said, "Yes, Sadie Rose. We could sure use you."

Sadie slipped through the sheeting to her room and quickly pulled on her clothes. She hadn't been big enough to fight the last fire she'd seen, but she was big enough to help with this one.

A cold band tightened around her heart. Was she brave enough to face the raging fire and fight it? What if it won and burned her to ashes?

2

The Prairie Fire

Her heart racing, Sadie flung the pile of wet sacks into the wagon beside the cans of water, shovels, a rake, and the plow that Caleb and Riley had lifted in. Bay, Caleb's big mare, stood beside the wagon with her reins hanging to the ground. Sadie knew as long as the reins touched the ground, Bay would stay right there. Dick and Jane shook their harnesses, and the jangle of the chains hooked to the wagon echoed across the rolling hills. The light from the moon cast a shadow from the team and wagon. Wind brought an occasional smell of smoke.

Sadie glanced at the horizon and saw the far-off glow of the prairie fire, and she leaned weakly against the wagon.

Tanner whined at her feet, and she patted his head. "It'll be all right, boy. It will." Silently she prayed that they'd all be safe and would get the fire out before it did much damage.

"Let's go," shouted Caleb, ready to spring up into the wagon. On his right hip he carried his Colt .45 and on his left hip his bone-handled Bowie knife. A wide-brimmed hat covered his dark hair and shadowed his brilliant blue eyes.

"Wait!" Momma ran from the sod house with Web, Opal, and Helen behind her.

Sadie turned with a frown. Would Momma make her stay home?

"What is it, Bess?" asked Caleb, circling her sturdy body with his strong arm.

"We're goin' with you, Caleb."

Sadie bit back a gasp of surprise. She waited for Caleb to order Momma back inside the way Pa would've done.

"Get in," said Caleb.

Sadie shot a look at Riley, and he was as surprised as she.

Momma had pulled the tail of the back of her calico dress up through her legs and tucked it in at her waist to make it easy to walk and work. "I'm ready," said Momma in her firm way. She retied her bonnet and retucked her dress tail.

With a smug look Opal walked past Sadie and climbed into the back of the wagon. She was tired of being left behind when exciting things happened.

"Yahoo!" shouted Web as he climbed up the wheel and jumped in beside Opal.

"This is not a picnic, Web," said Opal.

He grinned. "I know."

Helen ran to Sadie's side, caught her hand, and pumped it up and down. "We're gonna help fight the fire too. I can help...Momma said."

"Don't get close to the fire and get burned. I mean it, Helen!" said Sadie in a low, tight voice. After Pa had frozen in the blizzard, she'd taken his place to see that Web and Helen did their chores and obeyed Momma. Since Momma had married Caleb, Momma had told her not to boss the others around, but it wasn't always easy to remember.

Helen tossed her head and jumped up on the wheel. "I won't get burned. Not one bit. I'm eight, and I'm not a baby."

Sadie watched Caleb help Momma up on the seat, then she climbed in and knelt beside Opal and gripped the side of the wagon. Helen crawled up close and leaned against her. Riley mounted Bay in one easy motion. Bay pranced as if eager to run, but Riley held her in until Caleb gave the word.

Tanner barked as if to ask if he could go.

"You stay home, Tanner," said Caleb. "Take care of the place for us." He glanced back and for a minute caught Sadie's eye. "God is with us, kids. He has angels watching over us. We'll be safe tonight, and we'll be able to put out the fire." He slapped the reins against Dick and Jane, and they stepped out, jerking the wagon behind them. Caleb urged them to a run, and the wagon rattled and rocked across the prairie. Bay ran beside them with Riley leaning forward in the saddle, wind billowing out his loose-fitting shirt.

Wind whipped Sadie's bonnet across her back where she'd let it fall. She gripped the side of the bucking wagon and watched as the glow of the fire grew brighter and brighter. Smoke drifted on the wind, filling the air.

Sadie heard the water slosh and knew it was slopping out of the cans and buckets. Would there

17

be enough left to keep the burlap sacks wet?

Several minutes later Caleb pulled back on the reins. "Whoa, Dick, Jane."

The horses and wagon stopped. No one spoke. Not one sound could be heard in the prairie that stretched on forever and ever.

"Let's get to work," said Caleb in his Texas drawl. He dropped to the ground and helped Momma out.

Sadie looked further north where flames leaped high, settled down, then leaped high again. She wanted to ask Caleb why he'd stopped so far from the fire, but she knew she couldn't question an adult.

"Sadie, unhitch the team," said Caleb. "Riley, let's get the plow."

Momma stood to the side of the wagon. "Web, Helen, come to me. Opal, help Sadie."

Sadie didn't need help. She'd unhitched the team lots of times. Without a word she let Opal unhook one side while she undid the other. Dick's reins filled her hands, and she knew Jane's filled Opal's hands. Together they walked the team to the plow, where Riley hooked it up. Caleb didn't know how to use a plow since he'd worked with cattle all his life. Riley had learned to plow as soon as he was strong enough to walk behind one. But he'd always wanted to be a rancher and not a farmer, and so he was glad when Momma had married Caleb and they'd moved west. Now Riley wore a wide-brimmed hat like Caleb's instead of his farmer's cap that he'd always hated. He wore boots like Caleb's instead of a farmer's heavy shoes. Most of the time he helped Caleb with the cattle and horses.

In the moonlight Sadie watched Riley walk the team and plow to the spot where Caleb sent him. Riley plowed a wide furrow, turning up damp sod.

Caleb had told him to plow three furrows. The furrows would be between the fire and the wagon, so the wagon would be safe.

Momma pulled out the wet sacks and handed one to Sadie, then to Opal, Web, and Helen. "Follow me." She strode toward the fire, but Sadie was sure she wasn't going as far as the fire. She soon stopped and turned her back on the fire that hungrily licked its way toward them.

Sadie shivered even in the warmth of the wind. How she hated turning her back on the terrible enemy!

Momma lit a row of small fires and with the garden rake pulled the fire toward the furrows Riley was plowing.

Sadie bit her lower lip to hold back the questions buzzing like a nest of bumblebees inside her brain.

"You kids watch, so the fire goes where we want it to. Opal, Sadie, guard the ends. Slap the fire with your sacks if it goes beyond the point I showed you."

Smoke curled around Sadie's bare feet and spiraled up into her nose. Helen stood beside her, and Web with Opal.

"Are we gonna burn up, Sadie?" whispered Helen, shivering.

"No." Sadie trembled. "Remember, we got angels watching over us."

"I sure hope they're big ones."

"They are." Sadie knew even though she was no bigger than a mite that her angel was big.

"I hope they know how to fight prairie fires." Helen stepped closer to Sadie. At eight Helen was only a few inches shorter than Sadie.

Sadie gripped her wet sack more tightly. Water

trickled down her arm, and the wind blew it dry.
Why was Momma building another fire when they
were supposed to be putting out the one already
started?

Riley's voice sounded loud as he yelled "Gid-
dap" to Dick and Jane.

Caleb called, "Bess, you take care of the backfire, and I'll go help fight the fire."

"You go ahead. We can handle it, Caleb."
Momma sounded as if they were working together
on the garden.

Caleb grabbed a wet sack, leaped on Bay, and
thundered toward the racing fire.

Sadie dragged her wet sack over a licking flame.
It died out, leaving a black trail that once had been
tall prairie grass. She walked along, carefully guard-
ing her end of the fire. Finally she understood what
they were doing. They were burning a backfire that
would stop at Riley's furrows. When the big fire
reached them, it would die a sudden death with no
dry grass to feed it.

A flame leaped up, and Sadie grabbed Helen's
arm and jerked her forward. "Helen, watch where
you step! You almost burned your feet."

"I did not! I was watchin'."

Sadie scowled at Helen, but didn't argue with
her. More fire leaped up, and Sadie felt as if her legs
would melt like candle wax. The crackle of burning
grass seemed loud in the vast silence. A spark landed
on Sadie's faded calico dress, and she jumped back
and brushed it off before it could burn a hole through
the cotton fabric. The ground felt warm to her bare
feet.

After a long time Riley finished the furrows and
walked Dick and Jane to the wagon. The plow lay

on its side, the shiny blade covered with clumps of sod. "Need help, Momma?" he asked as he ran to her.

"It's under control, Riley. Bring a bucket of water, and wet our sacks again."

Sadie slapped at the fire at her feet, then slapped again and again at the stubborn blaze. Ashes flicked on her feet, and she kicked them off. Tears filled her irritated eyes to wash away the smoke. Her nose ran, and she rubbed the back of her hand across it, leaving it smudged. She wanted to be away from the smoke and the fire and go home and curl up in bed beside Helen and Opal. She wanted a drink of cold water to wash away the dryness in her mouth and throat.

She glanced over her shoulder. The big fire was closer, and she was sure she felt its heat. Fear stung her fingertips. Would the backfire work? It was almost to the furrows, but it seemed to be burning too slowly to stop the fast-traveling fire.

"Riley, the wind changed!" Momma's voice rang out with an urgency that Sadie had never heard from Momma before.

Sadie gripped her sack more tightly and held back the cry of fear rising inside her. She watched the flames of the fire bend east. If the fire got away from them, their cattle and horses would be in danger, and the prairie grasses that would be mowed next summer for winter hay would be destroyed.

"What'll we do?" whimpered Helen.

Sadie patted her arm. In the moonlight she could see the fear on Helen's dirty face. "Momma will tell us." Was that calm voice hers?

"Riley, plow another furrow over there as quick as you can. Kids, we'll have to start a new backfire fast." Momma ran to the grass that reached to the calf of her leg and once again started a backfire. It seemed to take forever for the fire to start, and then the flames licked across the ground and leaped high into the air. "Wet your sacks again," said Momma, gasping to catch her breath.

Sadie dipped Helen's sack and then hers in a bucket, then ran to the spot where Momma told her to guard. Once again they herded the backfire toward Riley's furrow.

What would happen if Riley couldn't get the furrows plowed fast enough? Sadie trembled. She knew their fire would no longer be a backfire then, but would the dreaded prairie fire destroy everything in its path?

Just then Sadie heard voices from the other side of the prairie fire. Heat from the racing flames reached her and burned into her. Frantically she cried, "Momma, the fire's closer!"

"I know," said Momma in a tight voice. "Just keep your mind on your work." With her garden rake Momma pulled the backfire toward the furrow faster than the wind carried it.

"I'm scared," whispered Helen.

"Keep your mind on your work," whispered Sadie. Silently she cried for God to keep them from being burned in a leaping blaze like the grasses.

A few minutes later she looked over her shoulder again, and her breath caught in her parched throat. The fire was almost to the spot where the backfire had started. She grabbed Helen's arm and shouted, "Momma . . . the fire!"

Momma looked back. "Run to Riley, and stand on the other side of the furrows. Run as fast as you can!"

"Give me your sack, Helen," cried Sadie. She held both sacks in one hand and gripped Helen's hand with the other. Together they raced for the safety of the furrows. Suddenly Sadie's foot caught in a tangle of grass. Her body jerked, and she fell forward and crashed facedown to the unburned grass with Helen beside her.

3

The New Family

Grasses scratched Sadie's face, and the heat from the fire burned her feet. With a groan she jumped up and pulled Helen up with her. Her nerve ends tingled, and for a minute she couldn't move.

Tears ran down Helen's cheeks as she looked helplessly at Sadie.

"We'll make it, Helen!" Sadie gripped Helen's hand more tightly and leaped across the grass toward the damp, wonderful furrows. She wanted to run faster, but Helen slowed her down. The wind roared in her ears. A sharp pain shot through her foot from stepping on something hard. She kept running, but it felt as if she were going nowhere. The furrows seemed miles away instead of only a short distance. Finally she reached the end of the furrows and ran around them and stopped, panting and gasping beside Opal and Web. Helen fell to the ground, gulping air into her lungs.

"Did you see Momma?" asked Opal.

A shiver trickled down Sadie's spine. "Where is she?"

Opal rubbed her dirty hands down her dirty dress. "I thought she was right behind me and Web, but she wasn't, and so I thought she was with you two."

"She's not," said Helen as she slowly stood. "Oh, Sadie, do you think something terrible happened to her?"

Opal slapped Helen's arm. "Don't say that!"

Helen yelped and grabbed her arm.

Sadie stared in surprise at Opal, who had never hit Helen or Web no matter how mad they made her.

Opal hung her head in shame. She couldn't stand to think that something terrible could happen to Momma like it had Pa.

"Momma?" called Sadie, then louder: "Momma!"

"Here!" Momma called back. "With Riley."

Sadie looked through the smoke and saw the blur of Riley still plowing the last furrow.

"She's safe," whispered Opal hoarsely.

"You hurt me," said Helen, rubbing her arm as she looked accusingly at Opal.

Opal's wide blue eyes, so much like Pa's, filled with tears as she knelt down to Helen. "I am sorry, Helen. Please forgive me."

Helen thought for a minute, then shrugged. "I will. I always forgive, because Jesus wants me to."

Sadie watched the prairie fire race on up to the burned area, die down, and trickle across to the furrows. Suddenly the fire was gone, and wind blew the smoke away. As far as Sadie could see in the moonlight, the ground was black and burned with no tall, waving grasses. How many bird nests with baby birds in them were burned? How many frightened prairie dogs had hidden down in their homes until the danger was past?

Sadie bit her bottom lip and tasted smoke.

Caleb rode into view and waved his broad-brimmed hat in the air. "We're all safe, and the fire's out!"

"How'd it start?" asked Riley.

"The new neighbors." Caleb motioned toward the north. "They had a campfire and didn't watch it."

"Oh my," said Momma, but Sadie knew she really wanted to say that it was unheard of to do such a dumb thing out on the prairie.

Caleb slipped off Bay and dropped the reins to the ground. "The family's from the Ozarks in Missouri where there's rocks and streams and no prairie. They had to get back to their little ones."

"Let's get on home," said Momma, sounding very tired.

Sadie yawned.

"First we'll make a stop at the water tank and wash," said Caleb. "You all look mighty dirty. And come to think of it, so do I." He laughed and hugged Momma close.

Several minutes later Caleb stopped the wagon beside the water-filled tank. The windmill squawked. Cattle lay in the grass. A horse nickered, and Bay answered.

Sadie dropped to the ground beside the wagon. She smelled the wet ground around the tank and her own smoke-covered body.

Opal slapped the water and giggled. "It feels

funny to be taking baths in the middle of the night. And in a tank instead of our tub." Every Saturday they took turns taking baths in Momma's round washtub.

Caleb kissed Opal's dirty cheek. "You're a brave girl, Opal." He looked back at the others. "You're all brave. Now let's see . . . who's brave enough to climb in the tank and wash, clothes and all?"

"Won't the water get too dirty for the cattle and horses to drink?" asked Riley.

"I'll let the windmill run all night and pump clean water into the tank. It'll be just fine." Caleb pulled off his boots and socks and dropped them in the wagon. He unbuckled his gunbelt and laid it across the wagon seat. "Don't just stand there, you green-horns. Let's get clean."

Sadie jumped into the water that came to her waist, then gasped and shivered. "It's freezing!"

Helen squealed as Caleb eased her down into the water.

Soon everyone stood in the water, laughing and talking.

The bottom of the tank felt slimy as Sadie stepped away from the edge. Her teeth chattered. She knew she had to duck down under and get wet all over before she would feel warmer. Taking a deep breath, she bobbed on in. Water closed over the top of her head, then she burst back out. Water streamed from her hair and down her face. Wind blew against her, and she didn't feel as cold as before. She stuck her head in the water and rubbed her face with both hands.

A horse stepped close to the tank and snorted into the water. Sadie laughed and watched the horse walk over to sniff Bay.

Several minutes later Sadie sat in the back of the wagon with the others while Caleb drove toward home. She shivered in her wet dress, but she felt wonderfully clean.

At home Tanner barked a welcome and Bossie mooed from beside the barn.

Momma walked tiredly to the house. "Put on your nightclothes, and then hang your wet things on the line."

Later Sadie lay on her side of the bed, with Helen in the middle and Opal on the other side. For once Helen didn't chatter until she was told to hush. Opal yawned and patted her mouth. On the other side of the sheeting Web whispered to Riley, then was silent. Caleb and Momma talked quietly. Sadie closed her eyes and felt as if she were sinking deeper and deeper into the mattress.

When she opened her eyes again it was morning, and Momma was frying pancakes. The sun was already high in the sky. It was the latest Sadie had ever stayed in bed. She jumped up and dressed quickly in her blue gingham good dress. A tiny burn on her foot reminded her of last night's fire. Her stomach growled with hunger at the smell of the pancakes.

"Wake the others, Sadie," Momma called from the kitchen.

"I will." Sadie shook her head. How did Momma know she was the one awake and getting dressed? Momma had eyes that could see everywhere.

Sadie leaned over the bed and shook Helen and then Opal. "Momma said to get up, girls."

Helen jumped out of bed, but Opal stretched and yawned and curled into a little ball.

Sadie peeked into the boys' room. Riley was

already dressed and gone. Web sprawled across the bed, one bare foot sticking out from under the light blanket. "Time to eat, Webster." She tickled his foot, and he jerked it up. "Get up, Web. Momma said."

Web shot up and reached for his bib overalls. He longed for rancher clothes like Caleb and Riley wore instead of his farmer clothes. Caleb had said several days ago that when he sold some horses and cattle and they had cash money he'd buy new clothes for Web, the kind he wanted.

Sadie ran to the kitchen. "Morning, Momma."

"Morning, Sadie. You look all rested."

"You do too." Sadie smiled at Momma, then set out the plates, forks, and tin cups for milk. The butter that she'd churned yesterday sat on the plank that Momma had set across two chairs to use as a table until Caleb finished building one. "I hope that Missouri family knows enough now not to let a campfire get away from them."

"Experience can be a harsh teacher." Momma flipped the pancakes, waited until they were a golden brown, then stacked them on a plate that already held a pile of pancakes as big around as the plate. She dipped more batter onto the griddle. The batter sizzled against the hot fat, and holes appeared all over the pancakes. Momma flipped them over just as Opal, Helen, and Web walked into the kitchen. "Morning, kids. Wash for breakfast, and eat before the pancakes get cold." She stuck another cow chip in the fire and poured more batter on the griddle.

Several minutes later Sadie forked a bite of the delicious, firm, butter-and-sugar-coated pancakes into her mouth. She liked the way the butter melted and ran over the edges. When they had syrup, she'd smear thick butter over the hot pancake, then float it in sweet syrup. Sometimes they had sorghum, but she didn't like that as much as syrup. It had been a long time since they'd had either sorghum or syrup. She drank her cup of milk, cold from being kept down in the well.

After breakfast she helped with dishes, made the beds, swept the hard-packed floor, and skimmed the cream off the milk to make butter again today. Opal mixed some bread and set it to rise.

Helen burst through the door, her cheeks bright red. "Someone's comin'. One on a mule, others walkin'."

Momma patted her gray-streaked brown hair and smoothed down her apron. "Let's go see who it is."

Sadie followed the others out and waited near Momma's tree for the strangers. The man on the mule was so tall his feet almost reached the ground on either side of the mule. A long rifle lay across his legs. His head was covered with a tattered wide-brimmed hat with a big black feather stuck in the band. He wore heavy pants, a flowered shirt with loose sleeves, and a leather vest. As they drew closer, Sadie could see the four walking were all boys. Two were fine young men that Opal would want to meet, one was about Sadie's age, and the other younger than Helen. They all wore new clothes and even had on boots.

Helen stepped closer to Sadie and clutched her hand.

The man stopped his mule a few feet from them. "How do, ma'am, young 'uns." He pulled off his hat, the feather waving, and held it to his broad chest. He had coal-black eyes and thinning dark hair streaked with gray. "I'm Zane Hepford, yer new neigh-

bor. And these are my boys." He pointed to the oldest and went down to the youngest. "Ellis, Gabriel,
Mitchell, and Varden." As he spoke their names they
tipped their heads, but none of them smiled. The
three oldest had their father's black eyes and dark
hair, but the youngest had eyes as blue as the sky
and hair as red as the comb on a rooster. Freckles
covered his nose and were sprinkled across his
cheeks. "We came to thank y'all for fightin' the fire."

Momma smiled her sweet smile. "We're glad to
meet you. I'm Bess York, and these are four of my
children—Opal, Sadie, Web, and Helen, my youngest. Won't you sit a while? Web, water Mr. Hepford's
mule."

"Zane. Call me Zane."

Momma smiled and tipped her head slightly.

Zane slid off the mule and handed the reins to
Web. "You got a good-lookin' family, Bess York."

"Thank you."

Sadie noticed that the four Hepford boys kept
their eyes down and looked very uncomfortable. She
tried to think of something to say, but before she
could, Opal stepped forward with a smile.

Flipping back her nutmeg-brown braids, she
looked right at the oldest boy, the better-looking of
the two fine-looking young men. "I'm sure you boys
are thirsty after that walk. I'll show you the well so
you can get a drink of water."

Sadie wanted to run to the barn and hide, but
she followed the others to the well, which was close
enough to the house that anyone could've found it
without Opal showing them where it was.

"I'm Opal, in case you forgot. I'm fourteen. And
this is Sadie. She's twelve. And Helen. She's eight.
Web's nine."

The short, wiry boy grinned at Opal. "I'm Gabe, and I'm seventeen. El here is eighteen. Mitch is thirteen, and our red-headed Vard is five."

"Want to see our baby chicks?" Helen asked, smiling at Vard. For once someone else could be the baby. She got tired of being the youngest.

"We got baby chicks too," said Vard in his Missouri accent. "But I'll look at yers after I get a drink. I'm powerful thirsty."

Through her long lashes Sadie peeked at thirteen-year-old Mitch while they each drank from the dipper. Mitch was short for his age and not muscled like the two older boys, who were talking to Opal. He caught her studying him, and she flushed and looked quickly away.

Mitch laughed and tugged Sadie's brown braid. "You don't have to be scared of me. I don't bite one bit."

Sadie lifted her chin and tugged her braid from his hand. "I'm not afraid of you. Want to see the rattlesnake skin we took off a snake we killed?"

He shrugged and grinned. His dark eyes twinkled. "I reckon."

She led the way to the barn where the snakeskin was stretched on a board that stood with other skins that were drying. She jabbed a thumb toward the snakeskin. "There it is!"

Mitch whistled. "You wasn't kiddin', was you?" He studied it closely, then looked at her with new respect. "That's some skin."

She squared her shoulders and looked smug. "I know."

"You're not bad for a girl."

"Thanks." She grinned at him. "Want to be friends?"

He thought about that for a while, then nodded. "I reckon with us bein' neighbors and all, it'd be a smart idea."

"I hope you don't start any more prairie fires."

Mitch rolled his eyes. "I told Gabe he better put out the campfire, but he never listens to me. He thinks I'm just a kid."

Sadie could understand just how he felt. She stuck out her hand. "Welcome to Nebraska."

4
Sadie's Job

Sadie gripped her hoe tighter, and her mouth dropped open. Naughty arguments whirled around inside her head as Momma continued to talk. Once while they were in town Sadie had seen a boy sass his momma. Right now she wished she was as daring as that boy.

Momma leaned against her hoe and looked at Sadie. "It won't take you too long to teach Mitchell to clean and cook and sew, Sadie. His pa says he's a quick learner." Momma chopped off a tiny weed. "We decided it yesterday when they were here. Mitchell will be over yet this morning." Her dark eyes were shadowed by her bonnet. "They'll pay you cash money—not much, but some. Enough for you to buy a pair of shoes, maybe a pair for Opal too."

Sadie curled her toes in the soft, warm sand beside the row of string beans. A gentle wind teased the loose strands of her hair. She could use a new pair of shoes. Hers were too tight and by winter would be way too small. Maybe she could buy a pair of shoes and a pair of boots like Caleb's too. The heady thought almost took her breath away. Was there a child alive who had two pairs of shoes?

"Their ma died without a one of them knowin' how to cook or clean. Not even sew on a button." Momma shook her head. "It's a terrible shame, them being without a woman to do for them."

Sadie glanced across the prairie where Opal was picking up cow chips with Web and Helen. Maybe Opal should marry El and become the woman of the house. El had talked the least of all the boys yesterday, but he was polite and nice. Last night Opal had said she liked him the best.

With a smile Sadie bent down over the hoe. Since Opal had so many nice young men to choose from, maybe she'd leave Levi Cass alone.

Several minutes later Sadie stood her hoe in place in the sod barn, then walked back out into the bright morning sunlight. Tanner waved his tail and licked her hand. "I got a job, Tanner. A real job that pays cash money."

He licked her other hand.

"I got to teach that boy from Missouri how to do housework. You think Mitch'll like that even a little bit? He doesn't much like girls. But we had a good time yesterday, once he saw the rattlesnake skin."

Slowly Sadie walked to the house. Mitch had told her yesterday that they slept under their wagon. His pa had figured on throwing up a log cabin for them to live in when they got to their Nebraska homestead—only to learn there were no trees on the prairie, and that meant no logs. He was thinking on what he was going to do: pay for lumber to build a frame house, or make a sod house. She'd heard Zane Hepford talking to Momma about a sod house. Maybe all the neighbors would go to Hepfords' and build a sod house for them, just like they'd done for York's family. The Hepford family would have to do something before winter set in. Nobody living under a wagon could survive the blizzards and icy winds of winter. She shivered, remembering what had happened to Pa.

In the house Sadie looked on the shelf next to the stove at the cans of flour and sugar beside the baking powder. Since she'd planned to make biscuits for dinner, she'd teach Mitch how to make them. Or if Riley brought home prairie chicken or rabbit, she'd teach Mitch how to fry meat. Caleb had killed a badger a few days ago, and Momma had saved all the oil from it for frying. Would Mitch know about badger oil?

They had let the fire go out, so she'd have to start it up again. Would Mitch know even that?

She brushed a piece of fallen sod off the pan holder hanging beside the dish towel. She'd made the pan holder out of the same material that she'd used to make Holly.

"Holly!"

Sadie peeked out the door to see Momma walking along the rows of corn and potatoes. Maybe she'd have time to sew up the tear she'd seen last night in Holly's arm.

A few minutes later Sadie sat on the kitchen

chair near the window, with Momma's sewing basket on the floor beside her. She threaded a needle, kissed Holly, and started to stitch her arm. "This won't hurt, Holly. I'll be done in a minute."

From outdoors Momma called, "Sadie, Mitch is comin'."

"Oh no," she whispered. Frantically she knotted the thread, cut it, and stuck the needle back in place. She hid Holly under a few quilt blocks in the sewing basket, then set the basket on the chair so it would be handy for Mitch. Somehow she'd hide Holly back in her crate before anyone saw her.

"Sadie!" Momma called sternly.

"Comin', Momma!" Sadie patted her racing heart, took a deep breath, and ran outdoors. She saw Mitch and his little brother stop and speak to Opal, Web, and Helen. Vard stayed with the others and Mitch ran across the prairie to the yard, a white sugar sack over his shoulder. Tanner ran to him, barking. Mitch stopped and talked to him and patted his head.

Tanner stayed at his side as he walked over to Momma.

"Mornin', ma'am," he said.

Sadie thought he looked embarrassed, but she couldn't be sure.

"Morning, Mitchell. How's your family?"

"Doin' fine, ma'am. Pa sent over this sack of stuff for you and yer family." Mitch held it out to Momma.

She looked inside. "Thank your pa, Mitchell, but it really wasn't necessary."

"He thought maybe you'd like some of these women things that we got no use for since we got no woman at our place."

"Take it to Sadie, please. And thank your pa for me. We will be able to use the dress goods, and the shoes might fit Opal."

Mitch glanced around, caught sight of Sadie, and waved. Today he wore faded pants that were too short for him, a patched gray shirt, and no shoes. "Excuse me please, ma'am. I got to start gettin' my learnin'."

"Sadie is a good teacher. She's been showin' Helen how to do chores."

"That's good, ma'am."

Sadie watched Mitch tip his head to Momma, then run over to her, dust puffing onto his feet. Tanner trotted along at his side.

"Mornin', Sadie." Mitch pushed the sack into her hands, then with a grin looped his thumbs in his belt.

"Howdy, Mitch." She wanted to peek inside the sack and look at the dress goods and shoes, but she didn't want him to think she was overly eager. "I sure hope you're not mad about me teachin' you house chores."

He wrinkled his nose. "Naw. Why be mad?"

But she saw anger in his eyes and felt it as he walked into the house with her. "It really is easy to learn to cook and sew and wash clothes and clean," Sadie encouraged.

Mitch pushed Momma's sewing basket to the floor, and thread and a thimble fell out.

"Be careful!" cried Sadie as she carefully picked up the basket, stuck the thread and thimble in place, and made sure Holly was carefully covered.

Mitch plopped down on the chair and crossed his arms over his thin chest.

"Momma loves her sewing basket. She's had it for years, and she needs it, so you can't treat it rough." Sadie rubbed the basket. "You can't learn to sew without this basket."

With a dark scowl Mitch shrugged. "I'd rather skin a rattlesnake."

"I bet you would." Sadie lifted down the flour can. "But right now you can help me make biscuits."

Mitch sat forward. "Pa made biscuits the other night that I couldn't bite without breakin' a tooth. That's when he figured one of us had to learn some things."

"How come he picked you?"

Mitch jumped up and knotted his fists. Fire shot from his black eyes. "I'll tell you why! I'm small, and I don't have the strength the big boys have; so Pa can get along without my help. Vard's too little yet, and that leaves me to do woman stuff and take care of Vard all day too."

"I'm sure sorry, Mitch. But you won't be small forever. I can remember when Riley was your size. Now look how big he is."

His shoulders drooped, and slowly he un-clenched his fists. "How about you? You gonna grow?"

Sadie wrinkled her nose. "Momma says I might stay small. I take after her grandma." Sadie lifted her chin. "But I can do lots of things, even if I'm small. I make great biscuits."

"I reckon it won't harm me none to learn to make a biscuit you can bite into."

"Wash your hands and let's get to work."

"Yes, ma'am!" He chuckled as he washed in the washbasin and dried his hands on the thin towel.

She showed him how to sift the flour into the blue and gray bowl. He took the sifter and laughed as the flour sprinkled down into the bowl.

"Look at this," he said. He sifted flour onto his bare feet.

"Don't!" She stared at him—she couldn't believe what he'd done!

He sprinkled flour onto her feet too.

"Mitchell, don't!" She grabbed for the sifter, but he held it out of her reach and laughed at her. "Give that to me now!"

"Make me."

Red circles brightened her cheeks. She shook her finger at him. "You give me that right now!"

"Nope."

"You better." She grabbed for it again, but he pulled it away, and flour sprinkled down the front of his clothes.

She wanted to punch him, but she didn't. "Stop foolin' around, and give me that flour right now!" she said in a voice that sounded just like Momma.

He cocked his brow and looked at her. "What's wrong?"

"Never, never waste flour! Never!"

"But that was just a tiny bit."

Trembling, she pointed to the can of flour. "The flour we have in that can has to last until next month when Daddy goes to town. When we run out, we go without."

Mitch shrugged. "I didn't know."

"Now you do."

Slowly he held out the sifter. "Are you poor folk?"

Her head shot up. "No!"

"Why can't you buy flour when you need it?"

"We don't have cash money, and Momma says we don't buy anything unless we pay for it or trade for it."

Mitch brushed the flour off his shirt. "I'm sorry about . . . about this."

She hesitated, then handed the sifter back to him. "Don't waste anything. Not even a pinch of salt. Not one thing, Mitch."

"I won't," he said just above a whisper.

She sighed, nodded, and watched while he finished with the flour, baking powder, and salt. "If we had paper I could write down the recipe for you." The only paper they had was Momma's for writing to her family in Michigan. No one else was allowed to use it.

"I got paper. I always carry paper in case I think of somethin' to write down." He pulled a folded paper and a stubby pencil out of his pocket. He smoothed it out and handed it to her.

She held it to her and felt its rough grain and saw the lines across it. Someday she'd have paper all her own, maybe a whole pad of it, and she'd write down special thoughts that came to her. She carefully wrote the recipe in her neatest penmanship, then folded the paper and handed it and the pencil back to him.

Later she showed him how to make milk gravy to eat over the biscuits. Riley hadn't shot anything, so they had no meat for dinner.

After dinner she showed Mitch how to wash and dry the dishes. Heat from the stove dampened the hair at the nape of her neck. He dropped a plate that he was putting away, and it hit the edge of the stove and shattered.

Sadie blinked back hot tears. "You have to be careful, Mitchell Hepford! I mean it."

He hung his head. "I'm sure sorry, Sadie."

She handed him the broom. "Here. Clean it up."

Later she picked up Momma's sewing basket. "I'll show you how to stitch a seam and how to sew on a button next."

"No!" He backed away from her. "Tell me how to do the wash."

She walked to the wash house with him. Web, Helen, and Vard shouted and ran around in circles on the other side of Momma's tree. Sadie stepped inside the cool, dark sod house. "This used to be our house, but the neighbors helped us build our big one and so we store cow chips in here and do the wash here."

He looked around. "It's sure little. Back in Missouri we had a big cabin with lots of room. All of us boys slept in the loft."

"How come you moved?" She saw his face close up, and she knew she'd asked a question that was none of her business.

"We just did," he said. He pointed to the tub hanging on a peg. "Is that what you wash in?"

"We rinse in that. And wash in that. See the wringers on the side? We heat water in Momma's boiler and use a stick to stir the clothes around and lift them to the wringer. Momma says clothes don't get clean unless you wash 'em in boilin' water and use plenty of lye soap." Sadie lowered her voice. "But a while back I stayed over at Jewel Comstock's. She lives on Cottonwood Creek, and she was born in the oldest town in Nebraska. Anyway, I washed my dress in cold water right from the creek, and it came clean.

So if you have to wash in cold water, it'll work. But I'd better show you Momma's way or she won't think I did my job well."

"My pa says yer momma would make a fine ma for us."

Sadie nodded. "She would."

"Maybe my pa could marry yer ma."

Sadie frowned. "Momma's already married to Caleb York."

"I reckon so." Mitch hiked up his pants. "I sure would like a ma, so I wouldn't have to sew and stuff."

"You did good with the biscuits and gravy."

"I reckon."

Sadie showed him how to set up the tubs for doing the washing and showed him how to use the lye soap. The smell of the soap stung her nose. Outdoors she heard Cluck call to her chicks and Helen's loud laugh. "Let's go back to the house, so I can show you how to sew on a button."

He walked outdoors to the well. "Buttons can't be that hard to sew on."

"They're not. You're smart, and you'll learn fast."

At the well he filled the dipper, drank, then handed it to her.

She drank, glad for the cold well water on such a warm day.

"Sadie, come here!" shouted Helen excitedly.

"Let's see what she wants, Mitch."

"You go see. I want another drink."

Sadie ran to Helen, Web, and Vard. "What is it?"

"Toad race," said Web with a great laugh. He set a fat toad on a line he'd drawn on the ground. "My toad can beat theirs."

Helen set hers down. "We couldn't find three toads, so I'm sharin' mine with Vard. We call it Warty. But it won't give us no warts, Vard said."

Sadie laughed as the kids cheered on their fat, squatty toads.

Web's toad jumped over the finish line first, and he picked it up and kissed its head. "Thanks, Pard."

"Let's race 'em again," shouted Helen.

"Ours might win this time," said Vard, gently touching the toad's head.

"It will win this time," Helen announced.

"We got to be goin'," said Mitch. "Come on, Vard."

"But what about sewin'?" Sadie asked with a surprised look at Mitch.

"We'll do it tomorrow."

"We'll have another race too," promised Web.

"And Warty will win," Vard proclaimed with a wide grin.

"Get a move on, Vard." Mitch strode away, and Vard ran to catch up to him.

Sadie looked after them with a puzzled frown.

5

The Missing Basket

Sadie watched Helen and Web race Pard and Warty. She didn't dare shout one on and not the other, so she shouted for both of them. "Come on, Pard! Faster, Warty!" Her cries rang across the prairie as the toads hopped toward the finish line. Suddenly she remembered the sack of stuff that Mitch had brought, and she ran to the house to look at it before Opal and Momma got back from their walk.

The pile of stuff was on the chair, but the sugar sack was gone. Sadie frowned. "Opal! Now, why would she want the sack?" Because she was the oldest girl, Opal always thought she got first choice of everything.

The room had cooled down since they let the stove go out after dinner. Smells of sod covered any other smells. A fly buzzed around the window, which was hot from the sun.

Smiling, Sadie lifted the shoes and touched the well-oiled black leather and heels, which were as high as the heels on Momma's good shoes. Sadie measured one to her dirty bare foot and shook her head. Her foot was too small. Maybe they would fit Opal, and then she wouldn't have to spend cash money for a new pair. Next, Sadie held up the dress goods, four different colors. "Oh my," she whispered as she touched the soft brown fabric lying on top of the others. She'd never seen such fabric. It was fit for a lady of high fashion like she'd seen in Momma's book. She held up the other three lengths—green gingham, pink calico, and blue calico. "Oh my! So much beautiful material!" How could anyone have so much? It was too great a gift from Zane Hepford.

Would Momma make Mitch take it back once she saw just how much was there?

Sadie held the pink calico to her. "I want this one," she whispered. "Don't send it back, Momma. Please don't!"

Maybe she should hide the pink calico, so if Momma sent the rest back she'd still have hers.

She trembled at the terrible thought. She would never, never do anything so dishonest. How could she even think such a naughty thought?

With a sigh she folded the dress goods and stacked them neatly on the chair, then hung the tied shoes over the back of the chair. "Momma, please keep the stuff."

Just then Opal stuck her head in the door. "Who're you talkin' to, Sadie?"

"Oh, you scared me!"

"Who're you talkin' to?" Opal looked around the room. She spotted the dress goods and shoes. "Shoes! Just look at them! Momma said they might fit."

"Did Momma look at all of this?"

"She said she did." Opal measured her foot to a shoe. "It's a little big, but I can stuff a rag in the toe." She hugged the shoes to her, and her blue eyes sparkled and her face glowed. "Won't I look beautiful wearing these?"

Sadie shook her finger at Opal. "You are so vain!"

Opal stiffened. "No, I am not! I said I'd *look* beautiful, not I *am* beautiful."

"You're still vain. You know how Pa hated when you acted vain."

Opal hung the shoes back on the chair and took a deep breath. "I don't like to be vain, Sadie. Honest I don't. Maybe if I was ugly I wouldn't be so terrible."

Sadie saw the tears in Opal's eyes, and she felt bad. "I'm sorry I said you're vain. I really don't think you are. You will look beautiful wearing those shoes. And see the pink calico? You'd look beautiful in that." Sadie locked her hands behind her back. What if Opal decided the pink calico was for her?

Opal fingered it and nodded. "It takes my breath right away to see so much material all at once. It's like being in a store."

"I know. Do you like the green gingham? And feel how soft this brown is!"

Opal rubbed her hand across it and sighed. "Momma will want this, I think. But I like this one best. I always wanted a green gingham."

Sadie breathed easier. She still might get the pink. Hearing a sudden sound, she glanced toward the door. Momma stepped inside. "Just look at all this, Momma!"

"I'd like the green gingham," said Opal. "And the shoes almost fit."

Momma touched each dress length and the shoes. "I can't understand why they'd give all of this to us."

"Please let us keep it, Momma," said Opal softly.

Sadie stood very still and watched Momma's face. She could see that Momma wanted to keep the gift, but she struggled with her pride. It was very easy for Momma to give to others, but it was hard for her to receive, especially such a large gift as this one.

Momma held the brown material to her. "I will speak to Caleb and see what he says. If he says we should keep it, then we will. But if he says we should give it back, we'll do it willingly."

Opal barely nodded.

Sadie looked down at the floor. She could not bring herself to agree to willingly give it back.

Momma held the bundle out to Sadie. "Lay it on my bed out of the way, and then we'll start supper."

Sadie carried it to Momma's bed, laid the goods in a neat pile, and hung the shoes over the footboard. If they got to keep it all and if she got to have the pink calico, she'd start her dress immediately. Momma would help her cut it out, but she could sew it all by herself.

She glanced at the chest where Momma kept her sewing basket, and her stomach knotted. The sewing basket wasn't there!

"Oh!" She clamped her hand over her mouth, and her dark eyes grew big and round. Wildly she looked around the room. The sheets were pulled back, so it was once again one large room with three beds in it. The sewing basket wasn't in sight.

She remembered then that she'd left the sewing basket on the chair in the kitchen. Holly was still inside it! What if Opal or Momma opened the sewing basket to work on the quilt blocks? What if they saw Holly?

Sadie's face burned. She heard Momma and Opal talking about supper. Tugging at the neckline of her dress, she slowly walked into the kitchen. Both chairs were empty. She stood near the window and frantically looked around. The sewing basket was not in the kitchen. Had Momma or Opal put it somewhere? She didn't dare ask about it, or Momma would scold her for not putting it back where it belonged.

She had to find it!

Without the sewing basket they had no needles, no thread, and no scissors. Without the sewing basket she couldn't sew her new pink calico dress.

And Holly was in the basket.

Sadie bit back a groan. Could anything be worse than this? Maybe Opal had hidden the basket just to make her pay for leaving it where it didn't belong.

"What's wrong, Sadie?" asked Momma.

Sadie managed a smile. "Want me to help with supper?"

Momma studied her for a minute, and it was hard for Sadie to stand still. Momma not only could see everything, she could sometimes read minds. "Milk Bossie and feed Babe. Give Babe only part of a bucket of milk."

Sadie nodded, and when Momma turned away, Sadie glared at Opal.

Opal lifted her fine brows in surprise.

Sadie flipped back her braids and ran outdoors

to get Bossie. Babe bawled from the corral that Riley had built to keep her away from Bossie. Babe hadn't wanted to be weaned, but Momma had said it was high time. Sadie had learned to stick her fingers down into the warm milk in the bucket in order to get Babe to drink from the bucket. Babe had sucked Sadie's fingers so hard, Sadie thought her fingers would pop right off into Babe's mouth. Finally Babe was able to drink by herself without the help of Sadie's fingers.

Sadie untied Bossie from her stake and led her to the barn. The barn smelled of manure and sod. Bossie stood quietly at the manger while Sadie sat at her side and milked her. Foamy warm milk pinged against the bottom and sides of the bucket. The sound changed as the bucket grew fuller.

A fly buzzed around Bossie, and she flicked her tail and barely missed Sadie's face.

"Where is Momma's sewing basket?" whispered Sadie against Bossie's dusty hide. "Where would Opal hide it?"

Bossie mooed as if she were answering.

"I'm gonna make Opal tell me what she did with it!" Just the thought of Opal seeing Holly made Sadie's blood turn cold.

She poured part of the milk in Babe's bucket and carried the rest to the house for Opal. "Where's Momma?"

"In the outhouse. Why?" Opal poured the milk from the bucket into another bucket that was covered with a cloth. The milk ran through, but the dirt and hair stayed on the cloth.

Sadie glanced around the room again. "Did you move Momma's sewing basket from the chair?"

Opal set the empty bucket on the floor and

looked at the two chairs. "I didn't even see her basket. Why?"

"No reason." Sadie's heart sank. That meant Momma had found it and moved it. If Opal had, Sadie would've been able to tell by the look on her face. When Opal was guilty, she got a very innocent look on her face that gave her away every time.

"Ask Momma, Sadie. She'll be back in a minute."

"I have to feed Babe and water Bossie and stake her out again." Sadie ran to the barn and carried the other bucket of milk to Babe. Sadie held it tightly against her legs while Babe drank. The calf butted her head against the inside of the bucket, almost knocking Sadie over, then drank more. Foam covered Babe's nose, and she licked at it with her rough tongue.

"Here, Tanner." Sadie tipped the bucket down for Tanner to lap the tiny bit of milk that Babe couldn't get out.

Tanner licked at the bucket until Sadie lifted it up.

Web and Helen called to each other as they ran around the house. At the well Sadie rinsed the bucket, filled it with water, and carried it to Bossie, then filled it again and carried it to Babe. Sadie staked Bossie out to graze until almost dark when Web would put her in the barn for the night. Soon Riley would finish the corral for Bossie, so she wouldn't have to be staked out.

Sadie walked slowly back to the house, her head down. What would Momma say to her for leaving the sewing basket out? She waited all through supper and after dishes were done, but Momma didn't say a word about the basket. Tension mounted in

Sadie, and she wanted to scream at Momma that she was sorry that she hadn't put the sewing basket away. But she clamped her mouth closed and wouldn't let the words past the lump in her throat.

Outside the open door, night birds called and coyotes howled. Caleb lifted his guitar off the peg where it hung by its strap. He set one foot on a chair and rested his guitar against his leg as he tuned it.

For once the sound irritated Sadie, and she turned away and looked out the door. The moon wasn't out yet, but a few stars twinkled brightly. A gentle wind pushed away the heat of the day and brought in a pleasant coolness.

Caleb strummed a few chords, then sang in his strong, clear voice, "Blessed assurance, Jesus is mine."

The others joined in, and finally Sadie did too, so nobody would ask her what was wrong. She usually enjoyed the evenings of singing and Bible reading, but tonight it was hard to listen, and harder still to sing.

The music rolled out the open door and across the yard to the vast prairie. Even the coyotes and the night birds were quiet for a while.

After prayer time Caleb hung his guitar back on the peg, then turned with a smile. "I hear y'all got a gift from our Missouri neighbors."

"We did! We did!" cried Helen as she caught Caleb's big hand and jumped up and down. She'd picked out the blue calico as her favorite, and she wanted to help Momma start on a new dress right away.

Caleb looked right at Sadie and she nodded, but she couldn't smile. Right now she could only think about the missing basket.

"I'll let your momma tell you our decision," said Caleb, winking at Momma.

She blushed, settled back in her chair, and smoothed down her dress. "Why don't you tell them, Caleb?"

Caleb boosted Helen up in his arms and held her tight. "We decided that y'all can keep the gift from Zane Hepford."

"Hooray!" shouted Helen.

Opal clapped her hands. "When can we start sewing, Momma?"

Sadie forced a smile, but butterflies fluttered so hard in her stomach that she thought she was going to get sick.

"We'll start tomorrow," said Momma. "We'll use the brown to make shirts for the boys, and you girls can choose what you want."

"Blue calico," said Helen at the exact same time that Opal said, "Green gingham."

"That leaves the pink calico for you, Sadie," said Momma.

"That's what I wanted," said Sadie in a weak voice.

"What about you, Momma?" asked Opal. "You need a new dress too."

"There's enough so that I can share Helen's." Momma folded her hands and looked satisfied. "We must all thank Zane Hepford for his kindness when next we see him." She turned to Sadie. "Tomorrow when Mitchell comes, you teach him how to bake bread and then send three loaves home with him."

"I will, Momma." Sadie wanted to run out into the night and hide from everyone.

"Momma, do we have enough thread for all the sewin'?" asked Opal.

Sadie froze. Had Opal asked that because she had hidden the basket and now she wanted Sadie to get scolded?

Momma nodded. "I'm sure we do. Helen, run and get the sewing basket and we'll check."

Sadie locked her icy fingers together and waited for the terrible announcement.

Helen ran into the bedroom. "Where is it, Momma?"

"On my chest, Helen."

Sadie trembled.

"It's not here, Momma," Helen called. She ran back and stood in the doorway. "Where else should I look?"

Sadie was sure everyone could hear the pounding of her heart.

Momma frowned and turned her dark eyes on Sadie. "Did you show Mitchell how to sew on a button today?"

Sadie shook her head. No words could get past the terrible lump in her throat.

"Opal?" Momma cocked her dark brows as she turned to Opal.

"I didn't use it today, Momma."

"Who did?" asked Momma, looking and sounding very stern.

Sadie swallowed hard as the others all denied using the basket. Finally she said, "I used it this morning, Momma, but I left it on that chair."

The room was so quiet, Sadie could hear the lamp flicker.

Slowly Momma stood. "Sadie, you know to put my sewing basket away after you use it. Did you hide it so you wouldn't have to teach Mitchell how to sew?"

Sadie shook her head. Tears burned her eyes, but she forced them back.

"What other explanation is there, Sadie?" asked Momma in a voice colder than any blizzard Sadie had ever been in.

Sadie hung her head. She had no answer.

6

The Wood Table

Sadie turned her head on her pillow and opened her eyes to find Helen staring down at her with an accusing look on her face. Opal was already gone from the room. Sadie jerked up, and her braids flipped over her shoulders. "Why did you wake me up?" she whispered.

"It's time to wake up, and Momma said to wake you up."

Sadie glanced out the window. She had slept late. Last night she'd tossed and turned and tried to figure out what had happened to Momma's sewing basket. She'd asked God to help her find it, and finally had fallen asleep with the moon shining in on her.

"Get up!" Helen tugged at Sadie's arm.

Sadie jerked free and rubbed her arm as if to rub off Helen's touch. "Leave me alone, Helen!"

Helen stood with her hands on her hips and her eyes narrowed. "You better bring back the sewing basket, Sadie Rose York! I want my new dress!"

"So do I! I don't know where the basket is. I think Opal hid it just to make trouble for me."

"No, she wouldn't do that."

Sadie moved to the edge of the bed. "And you think I would?"

"Web said you might, so you wouldn't have to help Mitch learn to sew."

"That's not true!"

Helen shook her finger at Sadie. "Then why did you hide it from us?"

Anger rushed through Sadie, and she jumped up and flipped Helen onto the bed. "Leave me alone! I mean it! Leave me alone!"

"Girls!" Momma's voice rang out from the kitchen, and Sadie hung her head in shame.

"Sorry, Helen," she whispered.

"No, you are not!" Helen slipped off the bed and with her back stiff marched out of the room. The sheet fell back into place behind her.

Sadie covered her face and groaned.

Later, while everyone else was outdoors, she searched the house for the basket as she swept the floor. She even looked in Momma's trunk where they kept all their oiled shoes so the mice wouldn't chew holes in them. She looked in the drawer where Momma kept her letters from Michigan and her five books and three fashion magazines.

"Where is it? Where?" She groaned in frustration as she stood the broom in the corner where it belonged.

Just then Caleb carried in long boards for the table he was building. "Grab that end, will you, Sadie

Rose? This cowboy can handle wild cattle, but it's hard goin' with things around the house."

Sadie helped him lay the boards down without bumping into the stove or chairs.

He started to walk out, then turned around and faced her. He pulled off his hat and worried the brim of it. "Suppose you tell me what is goin' on with you and that sewing basket."

She twisted her apron around her finger. "It's gone, but I don't know where it is. I really and truly don't. It's just gone."

"It don't have legs, and it can't walk off by itself. Who do you think took it?"

She brushed back a strand of hair. "Maybe . . . Opal."

Caleb rubbed a leathery hand over his jaw. "No. No, Sadie Rose. You roped the wrong calf there. I don't reckon Opal would tell us a lie and keep up that lie. You reckon she would?"

Sadie's shoulders sagged. "No. Opal wouldn't lie."

Caleb rested a hand on her shoulder. "Little Sadie Rose, I don't think you would either."

Her eyes brightened as she stared up at him. "I wouldn't! I really don't know where the basket is."

"I believe you. I reckon you got a real puzzler on your hands. It's up to you to figure it out. Just remember, you're not alone. God is always with you. He'll help you solve this, just like He helped you with other things."

Tears sparkled in Sadie's eyes as she flung her arms around Caleb just above his gunbelt and hugged him tight. She could smell the leather and sweat that was always part of him.

He kissed the top of her head. "It don't look like

that Missouri boy's comin' today. You head out and help Riley build the fence, and if that Missouri boy does come, you hurry back here to help him."

"But what about the basket, Daddy?"

"You keep on the lookout for it. You'll find it. Could be Tanner walked in and dragged it out."

Sadie gasped. "I never thought about that! Maybe he did! I'll look all over. He might've buried it!"

"You get on out to Riley. Maybe with the two of you workin' away, Bossie'll have a corral by dark."

Sadie smiled at Caleb, then ran outdoors into the hot sunshine. She looked for a sign of the basket as she crossed the yard, ran past the garden and Babe's corral, and stopped where Riley was digging a fence post. Dick and Jane moved restlessly where they stood hitched to the wagon, which now had posts in the back. Hot wind whipped Sadie's skirts around her thin legs. "Daddy said I should help you," she said.

Riley emptied the dirt from the shovel, leaned against the handle, and studied Sadie with eyes as brown as hers. "I thought you'd be lookin' for the sewin' basket."

She took a deep breath. "I did look, and I don't know where it is. Daddy said maybe Tanner dragged it outside and buried it." A sudden thought sent a chill down her spine. "Or it could be Tanner chewed it up." Had that happened? Was poor Holly torn to bits and scattered across the sand?

Riley rubbed a sun-darkened arm across his face to wipe off the sweat. "You better hope Tanner didn't do that."

Sadie nodded, her face as white as the clouds that dotted the wide blue sky. "I'm supposed to help you, and then I'll look around and see if Tanner took it." She wanted to look around right then, but she knew she had to obey Caleb. "What should I do?"

"Grab a post off the wagon and bring it here."

She ran to the wagon, eased a post onto her shoulder, and carried it to Riley. He dropped it into the hole and told her to push the dirt in. While she did that, he walked to the next spot and dug another hole. He dropped in a post and called her to fill it.

Sweat trickled down her face and neck. Sand gritted between her teeth. She wanted a drink of cold well water, but she kept working until Riley called her over for a drink.

A jackrabbit stood tall, then bounded away. A flock of ducks flew in a vee across the sky.

Finally Web called them in to dinner. Thankfully Sadie climbed in the wagon and rode with Riley back to the house. She helped him water Dick and Jane, unhitch them, and take them to the barn out of the heat of the noonday sun. She washed at the well, glad for the cold water as she splashed it on her hot face and neck.

She walked beside Riley into the house.

"Surprise!" cried Helen, bobbing up and down, her thin white braids bouncing.

Sadie looked around for the sewing basket, sure that was the surprise. But no sewing basket was in sight. "What surprise?" she asked with a puzzled frown.

"The table!" said Web, pointing.

"It looks great," said Riley, touching the smooth wood. Sadie could only stare at it. It was the most beautiful table she'd ever seen. It seemed to stretch forever across the room. A bench stood on either side and a chair at either end. For the first time ever, they'd all be able to fit around the table.

"I will show you your places," said Caleb proudly. He walked to Momma. "Bess." He circled her plump shoulders with his strong arm and walked her to the chair at the foot of the table. "This is your place." He pulled out her chair and seated her, then kissed her right on the mouth in front of everyone.

Sadie blushed and looked quickly away.

"Opal," said Caleb, standing at the bench on Momma's left, "this is your place."

She giggled and slid onto the bench.

"Helen . . . right here." Caleb motioned with a flourish at the spot beside Opal.

Helen leaped like a little flea across the room and into her place.

"Sadie . . . here." Caleb smiled at her, and she walked to her place and sat down. She watched Caleb seat Riley and Web across the table. Then he sat at the head.

Sadie folded her hands in her lap and smiled. A bowl and spoon sat in front of her. Slices of freshly baked bread lay on two plates, with two pitchers of milk beside them. Her smile widened. Today they were having one of her very favorite meals—bread and milk. Happily she looked at her family. All of them around the big wood table made a beautiful picture that she knew she'd never, ever forget. It would be absolutely perfect if only she could find Momma's basket and set it back in place in her bedroom where it belonged.

Caleb bowed his head, and Sadie did too. She felt warm inside as he thanked God for the family and the table and the food.

"And help me find the basket," she mouthed

just as Caleb said amen. She dared not believe that Tanner had chewed up the basket and Holly, or she wouldn't be able to enjoy the new table and the delicious dinner.

Later, just as she finished eating, Tanner barked to tell them someone was coming. She turned slightly on the bench to look out the window, and saw Mitch and Vard walking toward the house. Once again Mitch had a sugar sack slung over his shoulder. Vard carried something too, but she couldn't see what it was. "Momma, may I be excused please?"

"You may, Sadie."

Sadie walked outdoors and waited near the well for Mitch and Vard. Finally she made out two dead rabbits in Vard's hand, and blood dripping on the ground. Tanner sniffed at the rabbits, and Sadie sharply called him away. "Hello, Mitch, Vard," she said.

"How do," said Mitch, laying the sack on the ground as he reached for a dipper of cold water.

"Where's yer little kids?" asked Vard.

"In the house. They'll be right out."

Vard held the rabbits as high as he could. "We brung you these. El shot 'em plumb through the head."

"You boys didn't have to bring anything," said Sadie. "You gave us a nice enough gift yesterday."

"I brought flour and some other food Pa said I should learn to cook." Mitch sighed loud and long. "My biscuits turned out like rocks last night. Pa said I better try harder."

"You'll learn." Sadie looked at the bulky sack. "Did you bring flour because I yelled at you for wasting ours?"

"Reckon so."

She flushed. "You shouldn't have done that."

"It's done." He snapped his suspenders and laughed. "We gonna learn to cook or what?"

She felt a lightness in him that hadn't been there before. "We can fry those rabbits you brought and make biscuits again." She remembered the sewing basket. "But we can't do any sewin' today."

He shrugged. "No matter."

"Yer kids still got them toads?" asked Vard.

"Sure do," said Sadie. "You run to the house and ask if they can come out and play with you. They might have to finish dishes first, but you can help them if you want."

After Vard left, Mitch said, "What did yer ma say about the broke plate?"

Sadie shrugged. "Those things happen. That's just what she said: 'those things happen.'"

"I brought a plate. Pa said to when I told him what I did. It's not like the one I broke, but it's all I had to bring." He reached in the bag and pulled out a plate wrapped in a towel. He unwrapped it and held it out to Sadie.

Her eyes grew almost as big around as the plate as she carefully held it. It was covered with tiny bright flowers with a shiny gold rim. "It's too beautiful, Mitch."

"It was Ma's favorite."

"What was your ma like?"

Mitch twisted his toe in the sand. "She died when I was no bigger than Vard. But I remember her. She told us stories and laughed a lot and sang. All the time she sang to us, me and El and Gabe."

"What about Vard?"

Mitch's face closed up, and again she knew she'd asked something that was none of her business.

"We gonna skin them rabbits today or what?" he asked, nudging them with his toe.

"Do you know how?"

His face turned as red as Vard's hair. "'Course I know how. You think I can't do a simple thing like skinnin' a rabbit just 'cause I can't cook?"

"Sorry." She held the delicate china plate to her. Just what secrets were inside this strange boy from Missouri?

7

The Race

Sadie watched Mitch pull a knife from his pocket and skin the rabbits as fast as Caleb had ever done it. She filled a bucket with water, and he dipped the rabbits down in it, rubbed them off, and lifted them out. Water streamed down from them and splashed into the bloody water in the bucket.

"Get me clean water, Sadie."

She flung the water out over the grass. The sand soaked it up immediately. She filled the bucket again.

He dropped the rabbits in it and rubbed his hands down his pants, leaving wet streaks.

Tanner dragged off the head and guts and buried them near the barn.

She watched Tanner throw dirt, and she thought about the sewing basket. "I'll be right back, Mitch." Her heart racing, Sadie ran to Tanner and looked at the spots that he'd dug before. "Did you bury the sewing basket and Holly?" she whispered as she dug in the loose sand beside him. Dirt wedged under her fingernails. She uncovered a few sandy bones. Her stomach churned at the smell, and she pushed the dirt back over them.

Mitch chuckled from just behind her. "You hungry, Sadie?"

She jumped up and faced him, her dark eyes flashing. "Are you ready to take a cookin' lesson, or are you gonna make fun of me all day long?"

He tipped back his head and laughed, and his white teeth flashed in his sun-darkened face. "Shall we cook Tanner's hidden treasure?"

A giant tear rolled down Sadie's cheek.

He peered closely at her. "What're you cryin' about?"

Frantically she brushed the tear away, but another one followed, then another. Flushing to the roots of her hair, she ran away from Mitch and out into the prairie. She heard him beside her and she ran faster, her feet flying over the sandy ground. But he stayed with her. From deep inside herself she pulled strength to run faster; she was determined to outrun him. Back in Douglas County she was the fastest runner around. She'd even beat the big eighth-grade boys every race since she was ten.

She ran around prairie dog holes and around hills and around blowouts. But still he ran beside her.

Anger rushed through her, and she ran faster. He stayed beside her. She heard him laugh, and she scowled.

She ran past the spot where she and Helen had fought off the coyotes. She ran past where she'd shot the rabbit that Mary Ferguson had carried away for her supper. Over the roar in her ears she heard the squawk of the windmill.

Finally her anger faded and her embarrassment vanished. But still she ran. No longer was she running away from him, but with him. It was a race, a fine race like she'd never been in before. She felt as if she could run forever. Excitement bubbled up inside her, she called for more strength, and she ran faster and faster until the hills around her were a blur.

Pain stabbed her side, and her lungs felt as if they'd burst. She ran harder, toward the spot where the great blue sky touched the green grasses of the prairie. Despite all this, Mitch ran easily, as if he were only on a short walk.

A trembling started in Sadie's legs and moved up her body, and she knew the race was over. For the first time in two years she'd lost a race. But what a race!

She stopped and sank weakly to the ground, her chest rising and falling. She pulled great gasps of air into her lungs. Sweat stung her eyes, and she tried wiping it away, but it was no use. Finally she looked at Mitch. He lay on the ground beside her, fighting for air. Sweat poured down his red face.

He lifted his head and looked at her, then grinned. "That was the best race I ever had," he gasped out.

She laughed, then coughed. "Yes! It was the best race I ever had too. You can run fast."

"You too." He sat up and weakly rubbed sweat from his face. "I never been beat before, not even by El and Gabe, and they're good runners."

"I don't think I beat you."

"I was all done in. You beat me."

"I was all done in. *You* beat *me*."

He smiled, and for the first time since she'd met him she knew it was a genuine smile. It lit up his dark eyes and brightened his face. "Let's call it even then."

"Even." She smiled.

After a long time he said, "Why did you run from me?"

She picked a grass and studied it carefully. "I didn't want you to see me cry."

He shrugged. "I seen people cry before."

"Not me. I don't cry much."

"Me neither."

"I cried some when my pa died."

"I cried when my ma died. I stopped cryin' when Gabe said I was too big to cry." Mitch looked off across the prairie. "I never really stopped cryin'. Just in front of anybody. I'd go to the woods and I'd climb a tree and I'd cry where only the raccoons and the possums heard me. They didn't care none if I cried."

Sadie watched busy ants crawl in and out of their hill.

"How come you cried today?"

She trembled and hooked her hands around her knees. "I was lookin' for something I lost." She took a deep breath. "But I didn't find it."

"That's too bad."

"I know." She brushed back the strands of hair that had pulled free of her braids. "I asked God to help me. Do you believe in God?"

"I reckon."

"Me too."

"I had an old coon dog once, and one time he got lost when we was out coon huntin'. I asked God to help him find his way back home without gettin'

ate by a bear. Two days later ole Lucky came runnin' home without a care in this world." Mitch smiled
as he remembered. "You ever been coon huntin'?"

"No."

"Nothin' prettier than the song of a hound what
treed a coon."

She listened to him talk about coon hunting in
the Ozarks, and it was as if she'd been taken right
off to a whole new world. She told him about mov-
ing across Nebraska and about finding a best friend,
Mary Ferguson. She told him about being treed by
Jewel Comstock's bull, and he laughed and said he
wished he could've been there.

Finally he looked around. "Reckon you know
where we are?"

She slowly stood and turned all the way around
as she studied the hills. "Caleb York told me how to
read the hills."

"I could do that back home, but here everything
is different."

"We named the hills." She pointed to two small
hills nearby. "You learn the shape of the hills and
the shape of the ones around 'em and you'll never
get lost." She told him about the hill Caleb had named
Ball and another one, Point. "I know from that hill
that our place is that way."

Slowly they walked back across the prairie to
the homestead. She waved to Momma and Opal
under the tree where they were watching Web, Helen, and Vard have toad races. Tanner lay beside
the bucket that held the rabbits, his head on his
paws, his eyes sad. Sadie knew he wanted to pull
the rabbits from the bucket and eat them or bury
them for later, but she knew he wouldn't do it.

"Good dog, Tanner," she said, patting his head.

She filled the dipper and drank it dry, then handed it to Mitch. He filled it and almost emptied it with one long gulp.

He picked up the sack of stuff and the plate. He sighed loud and long. "It seems we got some cookin' to do, Sadie."

She carried the rabbits into the house. The coolness was a relief after the hot sun.

Mitch set the sack of stuff on the table, then stepped back in surprise. "That is some table, Sadie."

"Daddy built it. And the benches. Here's my place." She patted the part of the bench that would be her spot from now on unless they had company.

"My pa's a good builder—when he gets around to it." Mitch reached in his bag and pulled out a sack of flour, a can of baking powder, some lard, and a sack of cornmeal. "Pa said for me to learn to make cornbread."

"It's easy to make. You can learn it fast." Sadie stroked the sack of cornmeal. They'd run out a while back, and she'd been hungry for cornbread.

Mitch leaned against the table and smiled at Sadie. "I was dead set against learnin' how to do anything from a girl. But I like you, and I don't mind a'tall."

A warmth toward Mitch spread through Sadie, and she smiled. "Thanks, Mitch. I don't mind either."

"I reckon I should tell you something."

"What?"

Mitch ran his fingers through his dark hair and stood it on end. "You first tell me you won't hate me."

"I won't hate you. What is it?" She saw the agony in his dark eyes and frowned. What terrible thing was he going to tell her?

Just then Momma walked in, and Mitch's eyes went blank and he grinned as if he didn't have a care in the world.

"How's it goin' in here?" asked Momma.

"Look what Mitch brought," said Sadie, showing Momma the plate and the other things.

Momma stroked the tiny flowers on the plate and ran her finger around the gold rim. "It's a beautiful plate, Mitchell. Too pretty to use. I'll set it up where we can all admire it."

Sadie listened as Momma and Mitch talked. Sadie knew Momma would never say anything in front of Mitch about the trouble with the sewing basket. Momma didn't believe in airing dirty laundry. When she said that, Sadie knew she meant that family problems weren't supposed to be told outside the family. Sadie bit her lower lip. She'd aired dirty laundry when she'd told Mitch about crying over Pa.

Finally Momma said, "I'll leave you two to your work. Tell your pa thank you for the things, especially the beautiful plate."

"I'll tell him."

Sadie watched Momma walk toward the garden, then she turned back to Mitch. "What were you goin' to tell me before Momma came in?"

He snapped his suspenders and laughed. "Who knows? Who even cares? I'll get the fire burnin' so we can bake us some cornbread and fry us some rabbit."

Sadie sighed and watched Mitch lift the lid on the stove.

8

Mary's Visit

The smell of baking cornbread made Sadie's mouth water. Frying rabbit snapped in the hot oil in the heavy skillet. Sadie watched as Mitch carefully turned over a browned rabbit leg. "You're doin' good, Mitch."

"Thanks." He wrinkled his nose. "I'd still rather be out huntin' supper instead of fixin' it."

Sadie grinned and leaned toward him. "Sometimes I feel the same way."

Outdoors Tanner barked to announce that someone was coming. Mitch dropped the fork on the plate and jerked off the apron that Sadie had given to him to use. Sadie ran to the door and looked out. Momma and Opal were already standing in the yard waiting for the company.

"It's Jewel Comstock and my best friend Mary Ferguson!" Sadie turned excitedly to Mitch. "You'll like Mary. And Jewel too."

Mitch started to turn away, then jerked back and stared at the approaching team. "There's a cow and a horse pullin' that wagon!"

Sadie giggled. "I know. Annie and Ernie. Annie's the cow. Jewel said she never told them they look strange together, so they don't know it."

The grease popped onto the stove, and Mitch ran back to turn the rabbit again.

Sadie opened the oven door, and heat rushed out at her. The cornbread looked dry on top and pulled away from the edges of the pan. She carefully gripped the pan with thick pan holders and carried it to the table to cool on the rack she'd set there. She sniffed deeply, with her eyes closed. "Ummm . . . it smells good."

Outdoors she heard Jewel shout a greeting in a voice that could be heard up into Dakota Territory. A few minutes later she called whoa to her team. Sadie's heart leaped at the thought of seeing Mary Ferguson again. It was close enough to suppertime that she knew Mary and Jewel would stay.

Mitch forked the rabbit onto a platter and moved the skillet to the back of the stove, away from the heat. "There's not enough rabbit for everybody."

"It doesn't matter. We'll make more cornbread or something." She beckoned to Mitch. "Come on out and meet Mary."

Mitch snapped his suspenders and grinned. "Lead the way."

They reached the wagon just as Mary dropped to the ground. Mary wore the dress Sadie had given her, and her feet were bare. Her brown hair bounced and almost touched her thin shoulders, and her blue eyes sparkled.

"Sadie!" Mary hugged Sadie hard. "You smell like fried chicken."

Sadie laughed. Mary smelled like dust, but she didn't tell her that. "It's fried rabbit." While Momma and Opal talked to Jewel, Sadie introduced Mary to Mitch and Vard.

"Sadie told me about you bein' treed by a bull," said Mitch with a grin at Mary.

Mary nodded and laughed.

"Want to see a toad race?" asked Vard, pushing the toad almost in Mary's face.

She squealed and jumped back. "Not right now, thanks."

Sadie turned to Web and Helen. "You take Vard and go play." They ran across the yard giggling and talking, and Sadie squeezed Mary's arm. "I've got a lot to tell you. Come in the house with me and Mitch, and we'll talk."

While they walked to the house, Sadie and Mitch told Mary about the cooking and housework lessons.

"I could teach you how to bake a cake," said Mary, smiling at Mitch. "Want to learn?"

"I don't know," said Mitch, slowly shaking his head.

Suddenly Sadie saw her chance to look around the yard for the sewing basket. "Sure, Mitch, you want to learn. Show him, Mary. The oven is still hot." Sadie lifted the stove lid and dropped in a few chips. Fire blazed up, and she stuck the lid in place and set the handle on the shelf where it belonged.

"Do you have enough eggs?" asked Mary.

"I'm sure there is," said Sadie. "Mitch knows

where everything else is. I've got to go outside for a while, but I'll be back."

Mitch looked helplessly at her, as if he was begging her to stay with him. She would've given in, but she had to grab the chance to search for the basket.

"I'll be back," she said again as she ran out the door. She saw Opal watering Annie and Ernie and Momma with Jewel visiting in the shade of the tree. Web, Helen, and Vard were shouting encouragements to their toads.

Sadie ran around to the side of the house and looked around the packed-down places and further over into the prairie grasses. A snake slithered near her feet, and she stood still and waited for it to leave. It was a blue racer, so she wasn't afraid of it. Momma said it helped keep the mice from taking over.

Wind whipping her dress, Sadie searched all around the house and out into the prairie, but she didn't see a sign of the basket or of Holly. Finally she walked back to the house with her head down and her shoulders drooping.

She stopped in the doorway and saw Mitch sitting on the table while Mary mixed up the cake batter. Anger rushed through Sadie. How could Mitch dare sit on their brand-new table? "Mitch, get off that table now! Don't you know better than to sit on the table?"

He crossed his arms and stayed right where he was. "I'm learnin' to bake a cake."

Sadie stood with her fists on her waist, her feet apart. "You were supposed to mix the cake up yourself, not just watch Mary."

Mitch shrugged and slipped off the table. He picked up a rabbit leg and bit into it.

Sadie grabbed for the leg, but Mitch held it out

of her reach. No one was supposed to eat until mealtime. "Mitch, what do you think you're doin'?"

He waved the leg in the air. "I brought it. I skinned it. I fried it. I can eat it." Mitch took another bite and chewed with his mouth open close to Sadie's ear.

Mary clicked her tongue. "You're such a baby, Mitch."

His face turned brick-red. "Who asked you to butt in, Mary Ferguson?"

She shrugged and looked unconcerned as she poured the batter into a greased and floured pan.

Sadie watched Mary carry the pan to the oven, then turned to Mitch and mouthed, "What is wrong with you?"

He leaned close and hissed, "You think I want everybody in the world teachin' me to cook? It's yer job. Not nobody else's!"

Sadie wanted to grab him by the shirtfront and shake him. "Don't be such a baby," she whispered.

Mitch grabbed the empty sugar sack and pushed the fried rabbit into it. Grease spotted the cotton sack. He looked at the cornbread, shrugged, and marched out of the house. "Vard, get yer tail over here! We're goin' right now!"

Sadie stood in the doorway, sputtering with anger as Mitch ran toward home, leaving Vard to trail along behind him. Finally she turned to Mary. "He is such a baby!"

"Who *is* he anyway?"

Sadie told Mary about the prairie fire, the visit from the Hepfords, her job that would pay cash money, and the gift of dress goods and shoes for Opal.

"But why can't Opal teach Mitch?"

Sadie shook her head. "Momma needed Opal to do other things, so that left me."

"I guess you can do it for cash money and a new dress."

"Want to see the material, Mary?"

Mary nodded, and Sadie took her to the bedroom and opened the drawer where Momma had put the dress goods.

"This is the one I picked out."

Mary fingered it longingly. "It's so beautiful. When will you start it?"

Sadie sighed and told about the missing sewing basket. "The worst part is, we can't sew our dresses until I find the basket. And, Mary, Holly is in the basket! Holly!"

"That's terrible! Poor Holly. I'm sure sorry, Sadie. I can help you look for the basket while I'm here."

"I just don't know where else to look." Sadie dropped to the bench and covered her face with her hands.

Mary sat beside her. "Don't give up, Sadie. Tell me again when you found it missing."

So Sadie told the story again.

Mary narrowed her blue eyes thoughtfully. "I wonder if Mitch took it . . ."

"Mitch?"

"He is not a very nice person, Sadie."

"Oh, he's all right. He was mad at me, and that's why he acted so bad just now."

"Could he have taken it?"

Sadie frowned and tried to think . "I don't know how. I would've seen it if he'd carried it off with him. It's too big to hide under his shirt." She jumped up and paced the kitchen. By the smell of cake, she knew it was almost done. She stopped in front of Mary. "Why would he take it?"

Mary shrugged. "Why'd he take the fried rabbit?"

"He was mad. And it really was his rabbit."

"Did he have a chance to take the basket?"

"No." Sadie threw up her hands "Oh, I don't know!"

"Think about it."

Sadie plopped down on the bench. "I just don't know!"

"Next time he comes over, ask him about the basket."

"He'd get mad if I accused him of stealin'."

"Let him get mad."

"He might quit comin' and then I wouldn't get paid." Sadie knew having Mitch come meant more to her than cash money, but she didn't know how to put it into words.

"What'll you do with your money, Sadie?"

"I wish I could buy a whole tablet of paper just my own, and new shoes, and boots like Daddy's."

Mary's eyes shone. "If I had cash money, I'd buy dress goods for me and Jewel and shoes for both of us. I might even buy us a piece of candy each. Did you ever have a whole piece of candy just to yourself?"

"Once at Christmas." Her eyes dreamy, Sadie leaned back against the table and folded her hands in her lap. "That Christmas I got a doll I named Margaret and a piece of candy."

"What happened to Margaret?"

Sadie sighed loud and long. "Pa's dog tore her up when I left her outdoors one day. I didn't mean to leave her on the ground, but I laid her there so I could run a race with Riley. He won. And Margaret got tore to bits. I cried, and Momma said experience is a hard teacher."

"Did you get another doll?"

"Momma said I was too big. So I made Holly, and I tucked her away so nobody would ever see her and make fun of me." Sadie twisted her flowered apron around her hand. "And now Holly is gone too."

"You could make a new doll."

"No. Nobody could take Holly's place. Besides, I can't sew anything until I find Momma's basket."

The smell of the cake filled the room. Sadie jumped up and ran to the oven. She pulled the yellow cake out and stuck a broom straw in it to see if it was done. No batter stuck to the broom straw, so she knew the cake was ready. Carefully she set it on the rack on the table. "It looks good, Mary. And it smells delicious."

"It does, don't it?" Mary beamed with pride. "I bet smarty-pants Mitch can't make one that good."

Sadie frowned. "He could if he wanted to."

Mary shook her finger at Sadie. "You like him, don't you?"

"Sure I do."

"No. I mean, you like him the way you do Levi Cass."

"I do not!" Sadie shook her head at such a terrible idea. "That's an awful thing to say!"

"Why?"

"I don't know. Mitch is like . . . like Riley or Web to me."

Mary giggled. "If you say so."

"I say so!" Sadie stomped to the fire and dropped

in a few chips. "I got to get supper. Mitch was supposed to stay and help, but he didn't, so you can help."

"I did. I baked the cake." Mary giggled and poked at Sadie's arm. "You like Mitch...You like Mitch."

Sadie squared her shoulders and lifted her chin high. "He's a fast runner! And his ma died, and he cried for a long, long time." She pushed her face close to Mary's. "Are we gonna talk about Mitch forever, or are we gonna make supper?"

9

Momma's Basket

Sadie leaned her elbows on the table with her chin in her hands. Again last night she'd not slept well. She yawned. Soon she'd have to clean up the breakfast dishes.

Helen walked in from the bedroom and stood before Sadie with her hands at her waist and her eyes snapping with anger. "When will you find the sewing basket, Sadie? Look at this tear in my dress. Do you see it? Both my dresses need to be sewed up. And I want my new dress—I want it now!"

"Don't be such a baby!" snapped Sadie.

"Girls!" Momma turned from the stove and frowned at Sadie. "Sadie, I will give you one more chance to tell me what happened to my basket."

Sadie's stomach tightened. "Momma, there's nothin' to tell. I do not know where the basket is. I really don't!" She glanced away from Momma to see Caleb standing in the doorway.

He pulled off his hat and looked very thoughtful. "Bess, it's time we did somethin' about this whole thing."

"What shall we do, Caleb?"

Sadie curled her toes against the dirt floor.

"We will go to town and get new sewin' supplies. And we'll go today."

"Oh, Caleb!" Momma's hand fluttered at her throat. "That is too extravagant!"

"Bess, it's important."

"But we have no money."

"We'll trade for what you need."

Sadie saw the uncertain look on Momma's face, but she knew Momma would give in. She always did what Caleb said, just like she always had done what Pa had wanted. Momma believed that the man of the house was always right, no matter what.

Caleb kissed Momma's flushed cheek. "You get ready, and you and me will go to Jake's Crossing to get needles and thread and whatever else you need to sew them new dresses and shirts."

Momma untied her apron. "If you're sure, Caleb."

"I'm sure, darlin'."

"What will you trade, Daddy?" asked Riley. He'd learned that Caleb didn't mind his questions like Pa had. Pa had never allowed any questions, but Caleb had said, "How can you learn if you never ask?"

Caleb smoothed back the few gray streaks in his brown hair. He smiled, and his laugh lines deepened. "I'll think of something." He rubbed Web's head. "Maybe a good-sized boy."

Web giggled and shook his head. "You can't trade me for no sewin' stuff."

"You're right. We couldn't get along without our Webster." Caleb hugged Web tight.

Sadie sat on her hands to stop their trembling. Had she hidden the basket and forgotten that she'd done it? Everyone was so sure she'd done something with the basket . . . Maybe she had. Maybe her brain was all fuzzy like Jessy Ayers back in Douglas County.

Several minutes later Momma walked to the waiting wagon. Wind pressed her skirts against her sturdy body. She retied her good bonnet under her round chin. "We will be back before dark, children."

Sadie hung back and listened to the jangle of the harnesses and watched Dick and Jane swish flies off their backs with their long tails. A meadowlark sang from a fence post near the barn.

"Momma, will you really get needles and thread and scissors?" asked Helen, her eyes sparkling with excitement.

Momma nodded. "Daddy said we could."

"What did you decide to trade?" asked Riley.

Caleb stood with his hands resting on his gunbelt. "The rattlesnake skin and a few pounds of butter."

Web glared at Sadie. He'd planned on keeping the rattlesnake skin.

She turned away from him to look off across the prairie, but she couldn't forget the accusing look in his eye.

"You kids take care of things," said Caleb as he helped Momma in the wagon. "Stay at the house so your momma won't worry about you. We'll see you later."

Sadie watched the wagon roll away across the prairie toward Jake's Crossing. She wanted to run after Momma and Caleb and beg them to take her along, so she wouldn't have to listen to the kids' remarks about her and the sewing basket. Could she ever convince them that she hadn't taken it? There was sure no way her brain was just fuzzy, or the basket would've showed up before this.

Tanner licked her hand, and she reached down and hugged his neck. He smelled like old bones and dust.

Much later Opal called from the house, "Web, get a basket of chips from the wash house and take them to the house so I can bake the bread."

Web shot an angry look at Sadie, then ran to the wash house.

Sadie walked to the shade of the tree and looked toward the Missouri family's homestead. Would Mitch come today after his anger yesterday?

Tanner waved his tail and pawed her bare foot.

She patted his head. "I don't feel like playin' with you right now, boy."

He sank to the ground and rested his head on his front legs.

She sighed. Maybe she could kill another rattlesnake, so Web could have the skin. She knew he wanted to make a hatband from the skin to put around the wide-brimmed hat that Caleb planned on buying for him when they had cash money.

"Sadie! Sadie!"

She jumped at the sound of Web's angry shouts from the wash house.

"Sadie! Come here!"

A shiver ran down her spine at the frantic sound of Web's voice. She hesitated, then raced for the wash house.

Opal and Helen burst from the house. "What's wrong with Web?" asked Opal in alarm.

Riley ran from the barn, shouting, "Is Web hurt?"

Sadie started into the wash house just as Web was stepping out. He shoved against her, and she stumbled back into Riley.

"Look!" cried Web. His face was red, and his eyes were flashing with anger as he held up Momma's sewing basket. "Look! Just look!"

Sadie's mouth dropped open as she stared at the basket and at Web.

"Where was it?" asked Helen in surprise as she touched it to make sure it was real.

"Where?" asked Opal and Riley together.

"Ask her!" Web jabbed a thumb at Sadie.

Sadie gasped. "Me? I don't know anything. I don't!"

Web shook a white sugar sack. "It was stuck in this and hid under a pile of cow chips!"

"Sadie!" cried Helen, Riley, and Opal together.

Numbly she shook her head. "No. No."

"Daddy is tradin' away my rattlesnake skin for nothin'! Here's the sewing basket. Right here! And my rattlesnake skin is gone!"

"Settle down, Web," said Riley.

Sadie watched Web clasp the basket to him, and she suddenly remembered that Holly lay inside the basket. The color drained from Sadie's face.

"Give it to me!" Sadie grabbed the basket from Web and ran into the house. She scooped out Holly along with a few quilt blocks, dropped the basket on the table, and ran to her crate and pushed Holly deep under a chemise and a petticoat. She turned just as Opal marched in.

"What're you doin' now, Sadie?" asked Opal in a cold voice.

Sadie flipped back her braids and walked to the kitchen where Helen and Web were checking over the contents of the basket.

"I can't believe you'd do such a terrible thing, Sadie," said Riley.

"I didn't!"

"Who did then?"

She flung out her arms. "I don't know!"

"Momma and Daddy will be tradin' for stuff we don't even need." Riley rubbed a work-roughened hand over his dark hair. "I'm goin' after 'em to stop 'em. They sure don't want to trade when there's no need." He pushed his hat onto his head. "I hope I can catch 'em before they get all the way to Jake's Crossing." He grabbed the rifle from over the door and ran to the corral, whistling for Bay.

Opal smoothed down her apron and sighed. "Sadie, Sadie, when will you stop causin' so much trouble?"

"I don't like you no more, Sadie," said Helen.

Tears of frustration rose in Sadie's eyes, but she would not let them see her cry. Doubling her fists, she ran from the house and out into the yard. She ran past the well and into the prairie, past Bossie on her stake and past the rows of sod corn and potatoes.

She dropped down behind a grassy knoll and burst into wild tears. How did the basket get in the wash house? Why, oh why wouldn't her family believe her when she said she hadn't done it?

Finally the tears stopped, and she sat up and wiped her face with her apron. Hot wind blew against her, and the hot sun burned into her head. A hawk cried out and swooped across the wide blue sky.

"Who hid the basket?" she whispered around the lump that still blocked her dry throat. Her brain whirled with ideas.

"Mitch?"

She shook her head, then sat very still. What if he had? But why would he? "Maybe because he was so angry about being forced to learn," she whispered. She sat quietly, and the great silence of the prairie crept over her.

Just then she heard thundering hooves on the other side of the grassy knoll. It sounded like several horses. Was she in danger? Caleb had said to stay in the yard.

Carefully she peeked around the small hill and watched three riders race toward her very spot. She trembled and sank lower. She watched as the three men reined in their lathery horses and stopped just a short distance from her. She could see the riders easily, but she knew they couldn't see her. Their rough pants and loose-fitting shirts were dirty, their boots old and worn. Two men needed to shave, and the third was clean-shaven with a long handlebar mustache. He wore a wide-brimmed hat that looked brand-new, and the other two wore hats that drooped from long wear and no care. They looked about Caleb's age, maybe older.

The one with the handlebar mustache swung his leg up and rested it over the saddle horn. The boot on that foot was almost new and didn't match the other one. His spurs jangled, and his chaps flapped. "I say we give up lookin' for York and head back to camp if that place don't belong to him." He motioned to the sod house in full view. "We don't know for sure certain the man called York is the man we herded cattle with."

Sadie trembled. Caleb York had come from Texas and had herded cattle before he'd settled on his homestead.

"I want to find that sidewinder." The man wearing the leather vest pulled off his hat and slapped dust from his clothes. "But I say if that's not his homestead, we head back."

The other man swore, and Sadie's ears burned. "That better be York's place. If it's not, then them folks might know his whereabouts."

Handlebar Mustache said in his Texas drawl, "York's place or not, I could do with home-cooked grub about now."

"I could do with a drink."

"I could do with puttin' a bullet right through York's gizzard," growled the man who'd cussed. He patted the .44 at his side.

Chills ran over Sadie, and she sank lower in the grass. A piece of grass tickled her nose, and she felt a sneeze coming. She pinched her nose with icy fingers and waited for the sneeze to disappear.

"How we gonna do this?" asked Handlebar Mustache.

The man patted his .44 again. "Let me do the talkin'."

She watched as the men rode forward a little, stopped again, and talked a while longer, but the wind carried away what they were saying. They laughed and nodded, and she shivered again. Finally they kicked their mounts and galloped right for Sadie's home.

Weakly she lifted her head and watched the dust

rise behind the riders. "Oh, God, oh, God, tell me what to do!"

Opal couldn't protect herself and Web and Helen from the three men.

Sadie groaned. She could never run after Riley and catch him. And it was too far to go to Jewel's for help.

"The Missouri family!" It only took Mitch thirty minutes to walk it. She could easily run it in fifteen.

But could she get back in time with help before the men hurt Opal, Web, and Helen?

"Please, God, please put wings on my feet."

Sadie turned toward the north and ran like she'd never run before.

Help

Sadie's body burned with heat from the wind and the sun as she flew across the ground, still blackened from the prairie fire, and ran desperately toward the Hepfords' place. She forced back the terrible pictures in her head of what the three cowboys could do to her precious family if she didn't get help to them in time.

Up ahead she saw the flapping canvas of the covered wagon. What if no one was at the campsite? She pushed the ugly thought away and ran on.

She saw the dead campfire and the pot used for boiling water. She opened her mouth to call out when suddenly she stumbled and fell headlong to the ground, almost striking her head against the wagon tongue.

"I already promised not to tell the Yorks about Vard," she heard Mitch shout.

She opened her mouth to call out, but couldn't find the strength.

"You better remember that," said Gabe gruffly. "We don't want no trouble."

"What can't we tell 'em?" asked Vard.

"About yer family," said Gabe softly. "You know that."

The words buzzed inside Sadie's head, but she couldn't be bothered with the mystery over Vard when her family was in danger. She pushed herself up and managed to call, "Mitch, help me!"

"Who's there?" cried Gabe.

Sadie stumbled toward the boys as they walked into sight. "Help me. Please help me!"

Mitch sprang to her side and caught her arm. "What's wrong, Sadie?"

"Sit down and catch yer breath," said Gabe as he gripped her other arm and eased her to the ground in the shade of the wagon. "Vard, get her some water!"

Vard ran off, his red hair bouncing.

Mitch peered into Sadie's flushed face. "What's wrong?"

With ragged gasps Sadie told about the cowboys and about Caleb and Riley being gone. "I need your pa's help."

"Pa's off huntin' with El," said Gabe.

"I'll get 'em," said Mitch. "I know where they're at. It's further north on Sandy Creek."

"Thank you! Thank you! Please, please hurry!"

"I'll tell Pa to ride right for your place."

Sadie plucked at her skirts as Mitch sped away.

"Here's water for you," said Vard as he held out a canteen.

"Thank you." She gulped down the lukewarm water, then pushed the canteen back into Vard's hands. "I got to go now."

Gabe pushed her back down. "Not so fast."

"I got to!"

"Let Pa take care of it."

She shook her head, and her braids whipped against her face. "No, no . . . I have to go! I have to!"

"Whoa there." Gabe patted her shoulder. "What can a little mite like you do against three men?"

"I don't know!" Sadie looked wildly around. "Do you have a gun?"

He shook his head. "Pa and El have both of 'em."

She gripped her hands together and looked into Gabe's black eyes. "I can't stay here. Don't you understand? My family is in danger. I got to go. I got to!"

Gabe sighed heavily. "Then I'm goin' with you."

"Can you run fast?"

"I can, but Vard here's too little."

"No, I'm not! I can run fast. See!" Vard raced around in circles at top speed, then stopped in front of Gabe. "See!"

Gabe grinned and playfully slapped Vard. "I see, but yer legs are too short to keep up to me and Sadie."

Sadie jumped up, and her legs shook so hard, she almost fell. "I'll run ahead, and you two can come as fast as you can. But I can't wait around for you." Her legs shook harder, and she sank to the ground

"You're worn out from runnin' here. Rest a little longer and then go."

Sadie shook her head. "I can't wait!"

Gabe motioned to Vard to give her another drink, and she took it and drank again.

She pushed herself up and took one deep breath after another. Wind blew her skirts against her thin legs. "Are you sure your pa will help us?"

Gabe nodded. "He's never scared to stick his nose in other people's business if he thinks he can be of help."

"Here comes Mitch," cried Vard, pointing.

Sadie saw Mitch running toward them, his arms pumping. Shivers ran down her back, and butterflies fluttered in her stomach. She breathed hard as if *she* were running instead of Mitch. Finally he dropped to the ground in the shade of the wagon, his chest heaving.

"Pa and El are on their way," he said between gasps.

"Did they both ride Ears?" asked Gabe.

Mitch nodded.

Gabe turned back to Sadie. "Our mule can run fast, even carryin' double. So don't you worry no more."

"I'm goin' now. For sure."

Mitch jumped up. "Me too."

Sadie nodded. She could tell Mitch was tired, but knew that after a few minutes of rest he'd be ready to run again.

Minutes later, with Mitch beside her, Sadie lay in the tall grass a safe distance from her family's sod house. The three horses stood by the well, their reins hanging to the ground. Tanner lay under Momma's tree. He stood and looked toward Sadie, who whispered hoarsely, "Don't give me away, Tanner." She knew he couldn't hear her, but he settled back down anyway.

"The cowboys must be inside," whispered Mitch.

Sadie nodded weakly. Was Opal feeding them? Did she even know they were in danger? "Where's your pa?" Sadie whispered softly so her voice wouldn't carry.

"You can bet he's close by." Mitch kept his voice low too.

"I don't see the mule."

"Pa probably left Ears behind a hill out of sight. You can trust Pa. He knows how to sneak up on anything."

"Let's get closer."

"Tanner might bark," Mitch suggested.

Hoots and howls of laughter suddenly burst from inside the house and through the open door. A stream of swear words followed the laughter, and Sadie groaned. She heard someone bellowing "Old Dan Tucker" to the horrible twanging of Caleb's guitar. Muffled voices followed, and then Opal cried, "Don't do that!"

Sadie doubled her fists. What could be happening that Opal would shout at an adult in such a manner?

A pan clattered against the stove, and Opal shouted, "Leave her alone!"

Sadie bit back a scream. What *was* happening inside? What had already happened while she was running for help?

Helen squealed, and Sadie jumped up. Mitch hauled her back to the ground, and she plopped into the tall grass.

For a second she caught sight of Web at the door, and then Handlebar Mustache jerked him back inside. The door slammed shut, and the thud echoed out across the prairie.

"We have to get closer, Mitch!"

"We can't take a chance, Sadie, and you know it."

"I have to know what's goin' on. I have . . . "

"Look!" Mitch jabbed her arm, cutting off her words, and pointed at El.

He crouched low and ran from the side of the wash house to where the horses stood. He touched each one, gathered their reins, and walked them to the barn.

"What's he doin'?" asked Sadie.

"Makin' sure them cowboys can't get away." Mitch brushed a fly off his arm. "That El has a way with animals. He can talk to 'em. You notice how they went with him as quiet as lambs?"

Sadie nodded.

"He probably told 'em to keep real quiet." Mitch stiffened. "You hear screamin'?"

She shook her head. She could only hear the thud of her heart.

"Just listen."

She held her breath, and finally she heard the scream. "Helen," she whispered hoarsely. "Where is your pa?"

"He's here."

Frantically Sadie looked around. She felt more helpless than she'd ever felt in her life.

Just then she saw a movement at the back of the house.

Mitch jabbed Sadie's arm. "There's Pa!"

Sadie curled her toes in the sand and bit her lip to keep from crying out as Zane Hepford crept along close to the side of the soddy. Carefully he ducked under the window, then crept to the corner nearest the door.

El ran silently from the barn to the side of the wash house, his rifle ready.

Tanner lifted his head, but to Sadie's surprise he didn't bark.

Mitch whispered, "El and Pa will have 'em in a crossfire when they come out."

"I wish your pa would hurry," Sadie said very softly.

Just then Zane leaned his long rifle against the soddy, cupped his hands to his mouth, and howled loud and long.

A chill ran down Sadie's spine. The howl sounded just like a wolf. "What's he doin', Mitch?"

"It's an old trick. Them cowboys might think a wolf's after their horses, and they'll pile out of that house faster than you can say scat."

Zane howled again, then lifted his rifle and stood ready.

Suddenly the door opened, and the cowboy with the vest looked out. "The horses!" he shouted. "They're gone!"

"What?" cried the other two.

Sadie watched as the cowboys burst through the door, their guns drawn. White-faced, Opal stood behind them in the doorway with her arms around Web and Helen. Tanner barked.

"The horses!" cried Handlebar Mustache. He ran awkwardly toward the spot where he'd left the horses, the other two right on his heels.

Zane leaped around the corner and stood between the cowboys and the front door. "Drop yer guns!" Zane's voice rang out.

The cowboys froze.

Sadie jumped up, but Mitch caught her arm before she could run to the yard.

El shot into the air, and the sound echoed over the prairie.

"Drop yer guns!" Zane ordered again.

The cowboys dropped their guns and raised their

arms high in the air. Their chaps flapped, and the wind blew the loose sleeves of their shirts.

Zane glanced back at Opal. "Get back inside, young 'uns."

Opal pulled Web and Helen inside and slammed the door.

"What do you think you're doin'?" snapped the man who'd carried the .44.

"Is this the way you treat company?" asked Handlebar Mustache.

"No more talk from you. Keep quiet, or I'll have my boy fill yer mouths with yer dirty bandannas," said Zane.

Sadie jerked free of Mitch and raced to the yard. Tanner ran to meet her, his tail wagging.

"We got 'em," said Zane with a grin.

She nodded, not able to speak because of her great relief.

El kept his rife on the cowboys and didn't look at Sadie.

"I'll get a rope," she finally said.

"You do that," said Zane, chuckling.

Mitch moved to stand beside Zane, careful not to get between his rifle and the cowboys.

At the barn Sadie leaned weakly against the doorway. "Thank you, Heavenly Father," she whispered brokenly.

The horses snorted and swished their tails. Trembling, Sadie lifted a rope off a peg and ran back and handed it to El.

11

Explanations

With her hands locked together in front of her, Sadie watched El lasso the swearing cowboys, tie them together, and push them to the sandy ground near the well.

"You got no right doin' this," said the man with the vest.

"I told you not to talk!" Zane jabbed his rifle into the man's ribs.

"You gonna leave us right out in this hot sun and wind?"

"Not another word!"

"I'll get Ears," said El, handing Mitch his rifle.

Gabe and Vard stepped up beside Zane. Sadie hadn't noticed when they'd come.

She ran to the soddy and pounded on the door. The latchstring was pulled, and she couldn't get in. "Opal, let me in!"

"Sadie?" asked Opal fearfully.

"Yes! It's all right to open the door." Sadie heard Opal lift the latch and watched as she slowly opened the door. "It really is okay, Opal."

Tears stood in Opal's eyes, and her face was pale. She plucked at Sadie's hand. "We were so scared!"

"Not me!" said Web as he pushed his way past Sadie and Opal. He ran to Mitch and said, "Did you know they were bad guys?"

"Sadie told me," said Mitch.

Helen flung her arms around Sadie's waist and buried her face against her. "I was so scared! They pulled my braids and called me Cotton Top."

"They tried to take Daddy's rattles out of his guitar," said Web. He prized the rattles in Caleb's guitar as much as he'd valued the rattlesnake skin.

"I hung Daddy's guitar back up," said Opal. "I thought they were gonna break it. They did break a string."

"Did they hurt any of you a'tall?" asked Zane.

"No," said Opal.

"They pulled my braid and called me Cotton Top," said Helen.

Sadie kissed Helen's flushed cheek. "I'm glad you're safe now."

Opal brushed a strand of nutmeg-brown hair off her face. "At first they said they were friends. I didn't know they came to kill Daddy."

"It's over now," said Sadie.

"They made me feed them, and they sat on the bench and put their dirty boots right up on the new table." Opal wrapped her trembling hands in her apron.

"Someone's comin'," said Zane, lifting his rife again.

Sadie shielded her eyes with her hand and saw Riley ride toward them, Bay running flat-out. Caleb drove Dick and Jane at a full run, the wagon pitching dangerously. Dust billowed out behind them. Sadie felt the thud of the hoofbeats against her bare feet as Riley rode into the yard. The thud of her heart sounded almost as loud.

His rifle in hand, Riley leaped off Bay before she stopped. He landed with a puff of dust near the cowboys. "What's goin' on here?"

"They came to kill yer pa," said Mitch.

Riley stood over the cowboys, his rifle at his side. "You don't say!"

"Sure do," said Gabe with a laugh.

With Helen and Opal beside her, Sadie watched as Caleb pulled the team to a stop near the well. Dust filled the air, and Sadie coughed. Caleb jumped to the ground, then helped Momma down. She was covered with dust and looked frightened. Helen ran to her and hugged her tight around the waist.

"What's goin' on here?" asked Caleb. "We saw the yard full of folks, and we figured things weren't quite right." He peered down at the cowboys and whistled in surprise. "Boys, I never expected to see you again after that last run-in."

"They got no right to hogtie us," growled the man with the vest.

"Don't you believe it, Caleb," added Zane.

"Suppose you tell me what happened," said Caleb.

"I'll let yer girl do that." Zane patted Sadie's head, then looped his thumbs through his suspenders.

Sadie looked down at her dirty feet and then up into Caleb's piercing blue eyes. "I was out there." She pointed and couldn't look at Caleb. She knew she'd disobeyed and that he'd deal with it later. "They stopped close by me, and I heard 'em talk about you and say they wanted to shoot you through the gizzard."

Caleb listened as Sadie, with interruptions from Zane, told what had happened. Opal, Web, and Helen told their experiences too.

"Thank God you're all safe," said Momma.

Riley motioned at the cowboys. "Why did they want to kill you, Daddy?"

With his hat pushed to the back of his head and his hands resting lightly on his gunbelt, Caleb told how he'd ridden with the three cowboys when he'd worked for a Texas rancher right here in the Nebraska sandhills. "Lem Parker asked if I'd keep an eye out for rustlers. He knew how much trouble the ranchers had with 'em. I knew cowboys threw a wide loop from time to time in order to start their own spreads. I knew I'd have to keep a sharp eye on these three. That's Dandy." Caleb pointed to Handlebar Mustache. "And Tex." He'd carried the .44. "And Willy. These three were rustling and selling the cattle at the railhead in Ogallala, and I caught 'em. They were to be hung, but there was a fourth man helpin' 'em. Howard, it was. I wasn't there, but I heard tell that he came ridin' in, shootin' and yellin'. He set these boys free and they all rode out, not to be heard from again—'til now, that is."

Tex swore. "Howard didn't make it before I got a rope burn around my neck."

Dandy struggled to get up, but fell back down. His new hat lay almost under Bay's hoof. "You let us go and we'll head out and you'll never set eyes on us again."

"I reckon not," said Caleb coldly.

Zane pushed his hat to the back of his head. "Could be that fourth man is still around, seein' as how these boys are."

"May be," said Caleb. "How about it, Dandy? You up to your old tricks? Is Howard with a herd of rustled cattle in them hills out there?"

"You turn us loose," snapped Tex, cussing until Sadie's ears turned red.

Caleb jabbed Tex. "Shut your dirty mouth, mister. I'm turnin' you over to Joshua Cass, and he'll see you get to the nearest jail. You might get to that necktie party yet. We'll ride out in them hills and check on Howard. We'll be sure to give 'em your regards." Caleb turned to Riley and El. "Help 'em in the back of the wagon, and we'll deliver 'em to Joshua." Riley and El hauled the cowboys up and walked them to the wagon. Awkwardly they climbed in and fell in a heap on the wagon bed.

"Take 'em to the shade of the barn," said Caleb.

Sadie watched Riley lead Dick and Jane to the barn. With Vard's help Web carried water to the team, Ears, and the cowboys' horses.

Zane rubbed a rough hand across his jaw. His whiskers sounded raspy. "I'd be pleased to ride them hills with you, Caleb."

"I'd be pleased to have you." Caleb held his hand out first to Zane, then to El. "Thank you for comin' to the rescue of my family."

El didn't say a word, but he peeked at Opal. She smiled at him, and he blushed to the roots of his dark hair.

"Thank this little mite." Zane tugged Sadie's braid. "She ran to our place to get us."

Sadie flushed with pride. "I thank you too, Mr. Hepford."

"Call me Zane." He grinned and slapped his hat against his leg. "I reckon we're about even, what with y'all helpin' put out the prairie fire, and you, Sadie girl, workin' at teachin' that boy of mine how to do women's chores."

Sadie glanced at Mitch and saw the anger and embarrassment on his face.

Momma stepped forward with her nicest smile. "Could I offer you and your boys a bite to eat?"

Zane nodded. "Sounds good to me. How about it, boys?"

Caleb slipped an arm around Momma. "Them cowboys can wait a while longer. I reckon I'd like a bit to eat before I take 'em off to Joshua."

Sadie stood beside Momma's tree and watched everyone except Mitch and the cowboys in the wagon follow Momma into the house. Sadie smiled uncertainly at Mitch. "Aren't you hungry?"

He shook his head and hooked his thumbs in his suspenders.

She studied him for a long time. Wind ruffled his dark hair. "How come it makes you so mad to learn to do house chores?"

Mitch lifted his chin, and his eyes snapped. "I ain't no woman!"

"Nobody says you are. You're just doin' house chores for now. More than likely you'll have a woman in your house someday, and she'll do it all and you won't have to."

Mitch sank to the ground under the tree and picked up a leaf that had fallen. He curled his bare toes in the sand. "It don't seem fair somehow that I get stuck with it."

"Momma always says that a person does what he has to do, fair or not."

He nodded. "Reckon so. But I don't like it none. 'Specially sewin'."

Sadie stiffened.

"I remember my ma sewin', and I watched Carla Jean all the time too. Gabe said I was a real sissy for even watchin'. But I couldn't get over how they took a piece of cloth and cut it up in pieces, sewed 'em together, and out came a shirt." Mitch glanced at Sadie. "You think that's bein' a sissy?"

"No." She took a deep breath. "Mitch, did you hide Momma's sewin' basket under the cow chips in the wash house?"

He flushed and pulled into himself.

Sadie sighed. "You don't have to answer. I know you did. And I got the blame for it!" She thumped her chest. "You caused me a lot of trouble. Do you know that?"

He looked up, his eyes full of agony. "I'm sorry, Sadie. I started to tell you before. I sure don't want you gettin' in trouble."

"I'm already in trouble."

He hung his head. "Sorry."

"Because of that missin' sewin' basket, Daddy and Momma rode out today, then later Riley. Because of that, we could've all been shot dead by those rustlers."

Mitch groaned and rubbed a trembling hand over his damp face. "I don't know what to say."

"You can tell 'em all that you hid the basket and that you're sorry for the agony we suffered."

His face whitened. "I can't do that!"

"Why not?"

"I can't, Sadie. Do you know how Pa would feel if he knew? He don't need more grief from me."

"But what about me and my family?"

Mitch looked her square in the eye. Ears brayed, and Tanner barked. "Sadie, we got trouble you know nothin' about. It's all Pa can handle right now. I am sorry for makin' trouble for you. I truly am. But don't let Pa learn what I did."

Sadie locked her hands around her knees. Could she continue to take the blame for the missing basket? Could she take the angry words from her sisters and brothers, the accusing looks from Momma? An icy band tightened around her heart.

No! She couldn't take the blame any longer.

She opened her mouth to tell Mitch, saw tears in his eyes, and whispered, "I won't tell on you. I promise."

12
Holly

Sadie sat on the edge of her bed, bent over her slate, and wrote, "I don't like Opal at all. She is mean to me all the time. She has been very very mean since Web found the sewing basket."

Sadie frowned. The slate was full, and she wasn't finished writing. With an angry swipe she rubbed the slate clean with the rag she always used. Pa had bought the slate for her when she was seven. He'd paid two cents for it, and she'd promised to take good care of it so that it would last forever.

Someday she'd have paper to write on—paper that was hers alone. She'd never have to erase her precious words, but could keep them and read them again anytime she wanted.

The afternoon sun shone brightly through her window. In the kitchen the girls told Momma again what the cowboys had said and done as Momma cut out Opal's and Helen's dresses. Caleb, Web, and Riley had taken the cowboys and their horses to Joshua Cass. The Missouri family had gone home.

Again Sadie bent over the slate. This time she wrote, "Opal says I am mean. She says I took the basket just because I like to make trouble for her and the others. She is wrong!" Sadie underlined wrong five times, then wiped the slate clean again. She wrote, "I wish Mitch would let me tell the truth. What grief is his pa suffering?" She struggled over the spelling of suffering and finally left it. "What about Vard?" She wrinkled her forehead in thought. "Doesn't Vard belong to them?"

She stopped writing and sat very still, her insides jumping harder than Web's toad.

She read what she'd written, then wiped it off with the zip of her rag as if she were afraid someone else would read it.

Why hadn't she questioned Mitch further before he left with his family? Had he said all that stuff just to keep from taking the blame for hiding the basket?

She wrote, "He better be telling me the truth. If I ever find out he lied I will give him a BLACK EYE." She nodded. "Two BLACK EYES!!!" She flopped down on her feather pillow and looked up at the roots in the sod that showed between the planks.

"Sadie," Momma called.

"Coming, Momma." Sadie whipped the rag across the slate, stuck it in her crate, and ran to the kitchen. Helen and Opal wouldn't look at her. "Are you ready for me, Momma?"

"Yes. Spread your material over the table, and we'll cut out your dress."

On the bench beside the window Opal and Helen stitched their dresses carefully. They acted as if Sadie were a piece of glass that they could look right through.

Sadie gripped her dress goods tighter, then slowly spread it across the table, folding it where Momma said to.

Later Sadie blinked back tears as she bent over her new dress to sew yet another seam. Her hand cramped. She stuck the needle in the seam and flexed her fingers. Her heart cramped even worse, but there was no way to flex it to make it feel better. Could she continue to keep Mitch's secret and take the angry silence from Opal and Helen?

She sewed until it was time to milk Bossie. Thankfully she led Bossie to the barn and milked her. Bossie swished her tail across Sadie's face. Sadie rubbed her face against her shoulder and kept milking.

"Are you cryin'?"

Sadie jumped and almost tipped over. "Mitch! How long you been here?"

"A while. Vard went to find Helen. Me and Vard walked over while Pa, El, and Gabe went to meet with yer pa, Riley, and Web to see about them rustled cattle." Mitch kicked a clump of dirt. "I always get left behind."

"It won't always be that way." Sadie poured part of the milk in a bucket for Babe. "Want to feed our calf?"

He shrugged. "Reckon so." He took the bucket to the corral where Babe waited.

"I'll be right back." Sadie carried the milk to the house. Opal took it silently and strained it. Without a word Opal handed the empty bucket back to Sadie. As Sadie walked to the well and washed the bucket, a tear splashed on her wrist.

"You cryin' again?" asked Mitch.

She grabbed his empty bucket from him and rinsed it. "They all blame me about the basket."

"I'm sorry."

"Then let me tell."

He rubbed Tanner's ears. "I can't, Sadie."

"You're a selfish boy, Mitchell Hepford!"

"I know." He turned away, his shoulders slumped. "You can punch me if you want."

She sighed and shook her head. Slowly she carried the buckets to the wash house and hung them in place. She couldn't look at the pile of cow chips where Web had found the basket or she knew she'd take Mitch at his word and punch him hard.

"I hope Pa gets home before dark. I hate bein' alone with just me and Vard. I thought I heard a mountain lion or a panther last night."

"Maybe a bobcat," said Sadie. She staked Bossie out and patted her neck. "You're a good cow, Bossie."

"Do you always do the milkin'?"

"No. Web and Opal sometimes do. Helen's learnin', but her hands aren't strong enough yet." Sadie walked to Momma's tree and sat in the shade with Tanner between her and Mitch. She glanced at Mitch. "Who's Carla Jean?"

Mitch fell back, and his eyes grew round. "Where did you hear about her?"

Sadie frowned. "Why does her name scare you so much?"

"Who says I'm scared?"

"Is she part of your secret?"

"Don't even ask about her! I mean it!" Mitch looked wildly around, then leaned toward Sadie. "Don't you ever, ever say her name again!"

Sadie knew she should stop asking about his personal life, but she wanted to make him feel as bad as she did. "Is Vard part of your family, or did you steal him?"

Mitch leaped up, his breathing ragged. "You spied on us! Didn't you?"

She jerked him back to the ground. "I did not! If I'm gonna suffer because of your pa's grief, then I want to know what that grief is. You owe it to me!"

"I do not! You better not say one word to anyone about Vard or about Carla Jean. I mean it, Sadie."

She stuck out her chin. "Who would I tell?"

"Yer family. Jewel Comstock. Mary Ferguson." His voice rose, and he flung out his arms. "All the people in Jake's Crossing."

"Maybe I should tell them."

He looked as if he would burst into tears any minute, and she felt bad for being so mean.

She touched his clenched fist. "Will you calm down? I won't say a word."

"Promise?"

She sighed and nodded. "Yes."

He wiped sweat off his forehead. "Pa would skin me alive if he knew I told you our secret."

"You didn't tell me." She leaned over Tanner with her face close to Mitch's. "But I want to know everything."

Mitch shook his head. "You know too much already."

"You mean you really did steal Vard?"

"Don't!"

"I was only kiddin' when I said that."

Mitch jumped up. "I'm takin' Vard home right now. If you know what's good for you, you'll keep yer mouth shut."

Sadie scrambled to her feet. "Mitch, I already said I wouldn't say anything. You don't have to be so scared."

"We love Vard, and we're keepin' him. Nobody can take him from us. You hear me?"

"I hear you. And maybe Momma did too."

Frightened, Mitch looked toward the open door. "Do you think she heard?"

"I don't think so. She probably can't hear us over the noise Helen and Vard are makin'. But if you talk any louder she might."

Mitch licked his dry lips as he glanced toward the north. "I'm goin' home."

"Will you be back tomorrow? Momma says we're havin' Sunday Meeting here, and everyone's comin'."

"Pa will decide if we can come or not."

"I hope you do come."

Momma stuck her head out the door. "Sadie, where are my quilt blocks that were in my basket?"

"In my crate."

"I'll get them," called Opal.

"I'll get them," Sadie shouted quickly. Holly was in her crate—Opal would see Holly and show her to everyone! Sadie leaped forward and almost tripped over Tanner.

"Never mind, Sadie," said Momma. "Opal's getting them."

"Nooooo!" The cry rose from deep inside Sadie, and she felt like she would burst.

Mitch reached out to her, but she brushed him aside and ran to the door.

Momma blocked the doorway. Sadie tried to push past, but Momma caught her arm and held her. "Sadie, what on earth is wrong with you?"

Sadie strained away from Momma and looked around her arm into the house. She saw the looks of surprise on Helen's and Vard's faces. "Opal, you can't look in my crate!"

"Sadie!" said Momma firmly.

In anguish she looked at Momma. "Don't let Opal get in my crate."

Opal walked into the kitchen with the quilt blocks in one hand and Holly in the other. "Is this your doll, Sadie?"

All the strength drained from Sadie, and she leaned weakly back against the door.

Momma dropped her hands, looked at Sadie, and shook her head. "Sadie, you're making a terrible spectacle of yourself."

Opal held Holly by the back of her little flowered dress. She held Holly high and shook her slightly, then laughed and laughed. "Sadie has a doll!"

Laughter rang all around Sadie and seemed to fill her entire being. In agony she glanced at Mitch to find him laughing as hard as Opal.

Anger rushed through Sadie and filled her with a terrible strength. "Stop laughin'!" She lunged at Mitch and sent him sprawling in the dust as he cried out in surprise. She grabbed his coarse black hair, filling her fists with it, then jerked his head up and slammed it to the ground. "Stop! Stop laughin'!"

"Sadie!" Momma's voice rang out and penetrated Sadie's great anger. "Sadie, get up right now!"

Her body burned with shame and slowly she stood, her head down, her chest heaving.

"You apologize to Mitch this instant, Sadie York," said Momma in a voice Sadie knew she'd have to obey.

Without looking up, Sadie whispered, "I'm sorry."

Mitch didn't say a word.

Momma said sternly, "You go to your room, Sadie. Your pa will deal with you when he gets here."

Sadie walked into the kitchen. She glanced up at Opal and saw Holly still in Opal's hand. Weakly Sadie reached out for Holly.

Momma said, "No, Sadie, you will not take your doll."

Sadie's hand fell to her side. Slowly she walked away from the others and into her room. She sank to the edge of her bed and stared at her crate.

13
Forgiveness

Sadie lay on her side with her eyes wide open. She could hear the gentle breathing of Helen and Opal, and knew they were asleep. Momma had gone to bed, but Sadie could tell that she was still awake, listening for Caleb and the boys. Sadie knew Momma was trying not to worry about them being gone so long.

When Momma had said it was time for bed, Helen had asked, "Do you think that other cowboy with the rustled cattle shot Daddy and the boys?"

"Don't let your imagination run away with you," Momma had answered sharply.

Sadie had wondered if Momma's imagination was running away with her too.

Tanner barked, and Sadie listened without breathing. She heard Momma get out of bed and walk to the kitchen, and then she heard the rattle of the wagon and the thud of hoofbeats.

"They're home," she whispered, trembling. A while later Momma opened the door and quietly greeted them.

"You boys go right to bed," said Caleb. "You did a good job herdin' cattle. You're turnin' into first-rate cowboys."

Sadie could almost feel them puff up with pride.

After they were in bed Caleb told Momma, "It didn't take us long to find Howard and the cattle. He almost shot El before Zane got off a shot and hit him right in the chest."

"Oh my," said Momma in a weak voice.

Sadie shuddered.

"We buried him there, and then drove the cattle to my land. It was a good-sized herd. Most of 'em weren't branded, and cows had calves at their sides. I told Zane we'd divvy up the cattle without brands."

"That was nice of you, Caleb."

"Zane said he didn't see why he should get any cattle," Caleb continued. "But I told him it was only fair after what he'd done for my family, as well as him helpin' to bring the cattle in. I'm keepin' them all on my place until Zane gets his fences built."

Sadie closed her eyes tight and tried to force herself to sleep as they continued talking, but she still heard Momma say, "I want you to deal with Sadie in the morning. She went completely out of control over something and hit Mitchell Hepford."

"I'll talk to her in the morning before the neighbors come for Sunday Meeting. Let's get some sleep. It's almost midnight."

After they fell asleep, Sadie lay with her eyes wide open. Would she ever sleep again? Finally she slipped out of bed and looked out the window. The yard was bathed in moonlight. She walked to the kitchen, carefully lifted the latch, and opened the heavy door. She slipped outside, leaving the door open a crack so she could easily get back in. Tanner sniffed her and licked her hand. The sand felt cool and damp against her bare feet. Warm wind tugged at her nightdress as she walked across the yard. She pulled off her nightcap and let the wind blow against her warm head. Stars spread across the sky and reached down, down, down and seemed to sit on the distant hills. Coyotes howled, Bay nickered from the corral, and then all was quiet.

Sadie walked to the wagon and sat on its cold tongue, with her head in her hands. Would she ever be happy again? Would she ever hold Holly again and talk to her and be happy with her?

What had Momma done with Holly?

The hinges on the door creaked and Sadie jumped up, her heart racing. She watched Caleb step outdoors and look around. His unbuttoned shirt hung down over his pants. He ran a hand over his hair. She knew when he spotted her. She gripped her nightcap and watched him walk toward her. Would he say she needed a hard spanking? Would he scold her until she was in tears?

"Sadie Rose," said Caleb softly.

"Daddy?"

"Couldn't you sleep?"

"No."

He slipped an arm around her shoulders. "Too much on your mind?"

She nodded.

He sat on the wagon tongue and motioned for her to sit beside him. Tanner lay at their feet with his head on his front legs. "I intended to wait until morning to have a talk with you, but it appears I'd better do it now."

She trembled.

"First we'd better talk about you bein' out away from the house when the Texas boys rode up."

She moistened her dry lips with the tip of her tongue and stared down at the nightcap clutched in her hands. "I didn't mean to leave the yard," she whispered.

"Why did you?"

She took a deep, trembling breath. "Web found Momma's sewing basket hid in the wash house, and they all blamed me. I tried to tell 'em I didn't do it, but they wouldn't believe me. They still don't."

"Who did hide it?"

She bowed her head, and her braids slipped over her thin shoulders. "I promised not to tell."

He stroked her back. "Some promises are not wise to make, Sadie Rose."

She was quiet a long time. What did he want her to say? She curled her toes in the sand. "Do you want me to break my promise?"

He moved restlessly. "I don't reckon I do, Sadie Rose."

"Thank you." She watched a star zoom across the sky.

"I have a notion Mitch Hepford hid the basket."

Sadie gasped.

"I'd have to be pretty thickheaded not to think it was him since you didn't do it, Sadie Rose. You must have a big reason for keepin' it a secret."

"Yes, I do."

"You're a good friend to that boy, but I'm wonderin' if he deserves it."

She was wondering that too.

"You didn't say why you left the yard, Sadie Rose."

"I . . . I didn't want them to see me . . . cry."

"You could've gone to the barn or in back of the house. Never let your emotions get away from you and make trouble for you. It can be dangerous."

"I'm sorry," she whispered.

"It looks like we covered you leavin' the yard and the trouble with the sewin' basket. Now, we better talk about what happened this evening with Mitch Hepford. Why would a sweet girl like you want to black his eye? Was it over your promise?"

"No." Sadie's stomach knotted. "I got mad when I saw him laugh."

"What was he laughin' at?"

Her face burned, and she didn't know if she could tell him. "He just laughed to embarrass me."

"Out with it, Sadie Rose."

Her voice breaking at every word, she told him about Holly. "I know I'm too old for a doll, and I don't play with her much. Mostly I talk to her and tell her things that I can't tell anybody else. I didn't want them to laugh at me."

"I don't see why you're embarrassed about havin' a doll. If you want a doll, you go right ahead and have a doll."

"But they'll all tease me."

"I'll tell 'em not to."

She looked at him in surprise. "You will?"

He took her hand in his leathery hand. "You have to forgive 'em, Sadie Rose."

She stiffened. Forgive them? Never! She had every right to be angry with them. She had every right to hate them.

Caleb squeezed her hand gently. "You must forgive your Momma for not believin' you, the kids for being ornery to you, and Mitch for laughin' and embarrassin' you."

She closed her eyes tight. "I . . . I can't do it, Daddy."

"Yes you can, Sadie Rose. God lives inside you. Jesus wants to help you forgive."

She sat quietly with the wind blowing against her and thought about what Caleb had said. Her insides still churned with anger. "Daddy, I can't forgive them. I just can't. They don't deserve to have me forgive them."

"Sadie Rose, you don't have a choice about forgivin'. Jesus said you must forgive. He didn't say you could if you felt like it, or you could if it was easy. He said you must do it."

As Caleb reminded her about Scriptures talking about forgiveness, Sadie bowed her head and shoulders as tears rose inside her. Jesus said she must forgive, but she couldn't do it. She just couldn't!

Tanner licked her foot and whined.

Caleb sat quietly a while. The great silence of the prairie stretched on and on. "Sadie Rose, it's your decision. With unforgiveness in your heart, you block your communion with God. He don't hold Himself back from you, but you stop Him." Caleb leaned his head against hers. "You're a very obedient girl. You were taught to be obedient. I know you want to obey Jesus."

He stood and pulled her up with him. "I love

you, Sadie Rose. But as much as I love you, God loves you more."

She walked to the house with him, her heart heavy, a dark cloud over her.

Inside he rested his hands on her shoulders and looked into her upturned face. "Sadie Rose, in the morning I'm callin' a family meetin' before the neighbors come. I've let this whole thing go on too long. It's time our family started walkin' in love again. I'd planned on talkin' with you, but I see the problem is more than you." He leaned down and kissed her on both cheeks. "You go to bed. I'll see you in the morning."

She managed a nod. She couldn't speak, or she knew she'd burst into tears.

The next morning Sadie dressed slowly. She glanced at Helen beside the bed,

Helen stopped buttoning her dress and shook her finger at Sadie. "I always forgive because Jesus wants me to, but I won't ever forgive you, Sadie. You're a bad, bad girl."

Sadie opened her mouth to snap at Helen just as Caleb called them all for a family meeting.

"You're gonna get it now," whispered Helen with a naughty grin.

A muscle jumped in Sadie's jaw as she walked to the table and sat in her place next to Helen. She saw the smug look on Opal's face, and she wanted to run and hide.

Caleb looked calm and happy as he smiled at each one. Love for him welled up inside Sadie as she remembered their meeting last night.

Caleb winked at Momma, and she beamed with pleasure. "This is a wonderful morning, family, and we're gonna have a good time when all our neighbors come. I called this gatherin' so that we could get our own house in order. It appears there's been bickerin' and teasin' and all around unlovin' acts."

Sadie kept her eyes on Caleb. She couldn't bring herself to look at the others.

Caleb reached in his lap and held up Holly. "It seems like this cute little rag doll has been makin' trouble. This is Sadie's doll, and she can have this doll forever if she wants." He held Holly out to Sadie. "Here, Sadie. Don't be embarrassed over Holly. You did a good job makin' her."

Sadie slowly took Holly and held her awkwardly in her hand, then hugged her close. Oh, how good it felt to have Holly back!

"There will be no more teasin' that hurts others," said Caleb in a firm but kind voice. "It's fun to tease each other, but if it hurts someone it's no longer fun, and we won't allow it. Isn't that right, Bess?"

Momma nodded. "Yes."

Caleb leaned forward and locked his hands together on the table. "Sadie and me had a talk last night. She said she did not hide the sewin' basket. I believe her. She promised not to tell who did do it. I don't want any of you to cause her any more grief over it. We all love Sadie, and she loves all of us."

Helen burst into tears. "I'm sorry, Daddy. I was mean to Sadie." Helen leaned against Sadie. "I'm sorry, Sadie."

Sadie hugged Helen, and suddenly the anger toward all of them melted away. Without saying anything aloud she forgive them all, even Opal for making fun of Holly and for showing the doll to Mitch. Even if they kept being mean to her, she wouldn't be mean back.

"Can't we find out who did hide the basket?" asked Riley.

"Someday maybe, but not now," said Caleb. "I know y'all feel terrible for bein' mean to Sadie, but forgive yourself, and with God's help do better next time somethin' comes up."

Momma cleared her throat. "Sadie, I'm sorry I didn't believe you."

Sadie stared at Momma in surprise, then finally nodded.

Caleb talked to all of them about forgiveness and love and obedience. "I will not let my wonderful family fall apart over anything. This is a family full of love, and we want to keep it that way."

Sadie hugged Holly close and silently agreed.

14
Sunday Meeting

Sadie slowly tied her shoes. Company was coming, so they all had to wear shoes. She tried to wiggle her toes to ease the pain, but the shoes were too tight. She yawned and wanted to flop back on her bed and sleep. After the meeting with Caleb, they'd hurried around to do chores and to fix special things for dinner. Everyone was bringing something to eat to the meeting. After singing and Bible reading, they'd spread the food out on the table that Riley and Caleb had carried out under Momma's tree, and everyone would eat together.

Opal walked into the bedroom, her hair combed prettily around her shoulders. Today Momma had said she didn't have to braid it, but could let it hang down. Opal was very proud of her long, silky hair. She stood before Sadie with a sad look in her blue eyes. "I'm sorry for laughin' at Holly. And for bein' mean to you about the basket."

"That's okay, Opal." Sadie touched Holly where she lay on the pillow. No longer did the doll have to be hidden in the crate, but she could lay out on the pillow in plain sight of everyone.

Opal smiled, and her face lit up and once again her eyes sparkled. "I don't want to ever fight with you again."

"Me neither."

Tanner barked, and a mule brayed.

Sadie jumped up. "Hepfords are comin'."

Opal leaned close and whispered in Sadie's ear, "Did Mitch hide the basket?"

Sadie gasped and gripped Opal's arm. "Don't you dare say a word to him about it! I mean it, Opal!"

Opal loosened Sadie's fingers and rubbed her arm. "Did I say I was goin' to say anything to him?"

"You'd better not."

Opal shrugged. "I got more important things on my mind today." She sighed and clasped her hands to her heart. "Just think of all the fine young men that're comin' today. I won't have any trouble at all to get married when I'm sixteen."

Sadie rolled her eyes. "Can't you ever think about anything else?"

Opal's eyes clouded over. "I might."

Sadie ran outdoors to wait beside Momma for the Hepfords. Today the great sky was overcast, and the sun was nowhere in sight. The wind blew a pleasantly cool breeze. Smells of food drifted from the front door of the soddy. Sadie could see the feather bobbing in Zane's hat as he rode the mule into the yard. He carried his rifle in one hand and had a banjo hanging by a wide strap around his neck. Some

distance behind him walked El carrying a guitar,
Gabe with a hammered dulcimer, and Vard playing
a mouth organ. Sadie smiled. Today they'd have some
great music. She couldn't remember when she'd
heard any music except the music Caleb made with
his guitar. She glanced at Momma and saw the
pleased look on her face. Momma loved music almost as much as she loved Caleb.

Sadie frowned. Where was Mitch? Finally she
saw him trailing behind, a dot on the prairie.
"Momma, can I go meet Mitch?"

"I don't know," said Momma.

"Run along," said Caleb.

Sadie greeted Zane and the three boys, then ran
as fast as she could in her shoes that pinched her
feet. She wanted to take her shoes off, but she knew
Momma would scold her if she did. Momma said it
was important to dress for company, and that meant
shoes, even if they pinched.

She saw Mitch stop, and for a minute she
thought he was going to turn and run. He carried a
fiddle in his hand, and he was dressed in the new
clothes he'd worn the first time she'd met him. She
waved with her arm high in the air. "Howdy, Mitch."

He waited until she stood beside him before he
mumbled, "How do."

"Do you play the fiddle?" she asked.

He nodded. "You gonna punch me again?"

She grinned. "Not today. I sure am sorry, but
when I saw you laughin' so hard at me and my doll
I couldn't help myself."

"I wasn't laughin' hard."

"You sure were!"

He shook his head. "I smiled a little because
Opal looked funny waving that doll in the air."

Sadie fingered her bonnet string. "It looked to me like you was laughin' your sides off."

"I wasn't."

"Then I'm double-sorry for jumping on you. Did I give you a black eye?"

"No. And I made Vard promise not to tell Pa what happened, so he wouldn't ask questions."

They fell into step as they walked slowly toward the yard. Finally Mitch said, "I won't have a fit about learnin' to sew. I reckon if you can take a teasin' about yer doll, I can take a teasin' about sewin'."

Sadie laughed. "I reckon you can. I have Holly lyin' on my pillow. I don't care who knows about her."

"Maybe I can say that someday about doin' woman's work." Mitch groaned. "I reckon I have to learn it, embarrassed or not."

"I reckon you do." Sadie saw Jewel's wagon approaching, with the bachelors riding on either side. She had a lot to tell Mary! Joshua and Levi Cass were riding behind them. Would Levi take time to talk to her alone today, or would he be too tied up with Opal? Sadie shrugged. For some reason it didn't matter. "Mitch, this is a great day!"

Later singing and music from two guitars, two fiddles, a hammered dulcimer, a banjo, and Vard's mouth organ rang across the prairie. Near the table covered with food, Sadie stood beside Mary, and her was heart filled with love for her family and her neighbors. They were all here together, singing and loving, and it seemed like there was no one else in the world, not even out beyond the endless sea of grass.

As she sang, she watched Mitch play his fiddle. His face was lit up like a bright candle, and he tapped his toe as he played. Maybe he'd teach her how to play the fiddle.

She glanced at Caleb as he played his guitar and sang. He caught her look and winked. She smiled back and sang with all her heart.